"After Kate suffers a profound loss, she travels to the beautiful coastal town of Taormina, Italy, to meet her cousin Rosa for the first time. Together, they uncover family secrets, and through a series of 'coincidental' events, Kate finds compassion and forgiveness. *Under the Tropical Skies* is a powerful page-turner that will keep you up all night. Once again, award-winning novelist Maryann Ridini Spencer has a winner."

~~**Catherine Makino**
Award-winning multimedia journalist, Thomson Reuters,
the *San Francisco Chronicle*, the *Los Angeles Times*,
Voice of America Radio

"Maryann Ridini Spencer's *Under the Tropical Skies* has done it again! Another compelling Kate Grace must-read demonstrating the power of acceptance and healing through understanding oneself and the stories of others."

~~**Kimberly Anderson**
International Bestselling Author of *The Goddesses Among Us*
anthology books and workshops

Other Books by

Maryann Ridini Spencer

<u>Kate Grace Novels</u>

Lady in the Window
The Paradise Table
Secrets of Grace Manor

<u>Cookbooks</u>

Simply Delicious Living with Maryann®—Entrées

Under the Tropical Skies

a Kate Grace Novel

Under the Tropical Skies

a Kate Grace Novel

Maryann Ridini Spencer

Santa Rosa
PRESS
SantaRosaPress.net

Under the Tropical Skies
a Kate Grace Novel

First Edition, copyright © 2022
Maryann Ridini Spencer

 Under the Tropical Skies is a work of fiction. Names, characters, events, and incidents are products of the author's imagination or are used factitiously. Any resemblance to actual persons, living or dead, is entirely coincidental.

 Hardcover, trade paperback and eBook editions published in 2022 by Santa Rosa Press, publisher@SantaRosaPress.net.

Hardcover ISBN: 978-1-7362111-4-4
Paperback ISBN: 978-1-7362111-5-1
Ebook/EPUB ISBN: 978-1-7362111-6-8
Ebook/Mobipocket ISBN: 978-1-7362111-7-5

Library of Congress Control Number: 2022945307

Publisher's Cataloging-in-Publication data

Names: Spencer, Maryann Ridini, author.
Title: Under the tropical skies: a Kate Grace novel / Maryann Ridini Spencer.
Series: Kate Grace Mystery
Description: La Quinta, CA: Santa Rosa Press, 2022.
Identifiers: LCCN: 2022945307 | ISBN: 978-1-7362111-4-4 (hardcover) | 978-1-7362111-5-1 (paperback) | 978-1-7362111-6-8 (epub) | 978-1-7362111-7-5 (mobi)
Subjects: LCSH Friendship--Fiction. | Family--Fiction. | Journalists--Fiction | Hawaii--Fiction. | Love stories. | Mystery fiction. | BISAC FICTION / Mystery & Detective / General | FICTION / Mystery & Detective / Women Sleuths | FICTION / Romance / Christian Fiction/ Contemporary | FICTION / Romance / Historical / General | FICTION / Visionary & Metaphysical | FICTION / Women
Classification: LCC PS3619.P4655 U63 2022 | DDC 813.6--dc23

Book Graphics:

- o Hibiscus Graphic (before poems) – ©CanStock Photo/Kotkoa
- o Taormina Panorama and Ruins (front cover and before Prologue) – ©CanStock Photo/Pilat666
- o Section Break Lily – ©CanStock Photo/Evgeniia Hulinska
- o Hanalei Beach (before Chapter 2) – ©Maryann Ridini Spencer
- o Kona View (before Chapter 3) – ©Maryann Ridini Spencer
- o Single Lily (before Chapter 4) – ©CanStock Photo/David Carillet
- o Butterfly (before Chapter 10) – ©Maryann Ridini Spencer
- o Kona View (before Chapter 14) – ©Maryann Ridini Spencer
- o Wet Plumeria (before Chapter 21) – ©Maryann Ridini Spencer
- o Open Diary (before Chapter 24) – ©CanStock Photo/svl861
- o Taormina (before Chapter 25) – ©CanStock Photo/Pilat666
- o Woman wearing Hat – (front cover and before Chapter 26) – ©Adobe Stock/Olezzo
- o single flower (before Chapter 37) – ©Maryann Ridini Spencer

Edited by Jenny Margotta, editorjennymargotta@mail.com

Book Cover Graphic Design: Michelle Prebble, Michelle Prebble Designs, www.MichellePrebble.com.
Cover photos: Front cover: Taormina and Ruins, ©CanStock Photo/Pilat666 and Woman, ©Adobe Stock /Olezzo. Back cover: ocean and author photo, ©Maryann Ridini Spencer

Printed and published in the United States of America
10 9 8 7 6 5 4 3 2 1

Acknowledgments

It's easy to hold on to anger and resentment when we feel the world has wronged us, or life circumstances, a family member, a romantic partner, a friend, or a random act inflicts mental, physical, or emotional pain. Holding on to the upset and remaining the victim, or harboring the desire for revenge or payback, is also more destructive to the wronged individual than it is to the perpetrator.

Research shows that remaining in a state of unforgiveness (toward oneself or others) produces anxiety, PTSD, and depression. Holding on to negative feelings and emotions can also often lead to ill health. Conversely, forgiving creates beneficial psychological and spiritual states, fosters healing, reduces depression and anxiety, and increases self-esteem and physical and mental well-being.

When interviewed or discussing my work in television, film, and publishing, I always talk about *Aloha*, the beautiful Hawaiian word that rolls off the tongue. In the Hawaiian Islands, you use the word *Aloha* when you greet a person hello or bid them farewell. *Aloha* also means *love* and *affection,* and *Aloha*'s meaning also extends to an attitude or way of living life.

Living in *The Spirit of Aloha* or *The Way of Aloha* means interacting with the natural world and all those who live in that world by a specific code of ethics which includes but is not limited to love, kindness, tolerance, compassion, respect, and honor of all humanity and living things. Living *The Way* also includes the thoughtful and deliberate preservation of the earth and its precious resources, the joyful sharing of oneself with others, the act of being committed to the caring and the sustainability of one's community and the planet, and "conscious manifestation" to live life joyfully in the present. The list of meanings goes on, but clearly, *Aloha* means so much more than "hello" or "goodbye." The Hawaiians believe that when you "Live Aloha," you uplift the *mana* (spirit) of all our human *ohana* (family).

I interpret "Living Aloha" as living the way God wants us to live. I feel compelled to write themes of *Aloha*, whether the backdrop is modern-day Hawaii or another place and time in the world.

In *Under the Tropical Skies*, my character Kate Grace, through her circumstances and learning about others' experiences, comes face to face with what it means to practice forgiveness—toward herself and others as well as living in faith by yielding to God's will.

While researching and writing *Under the Tropical Skies*, I discovered and learned about the beloved Italian Saint Maria Teresa Goretti, an Italian virgin-martyr canonized on June 24, 1950, by Pope Pius XII and one of the youngest saints on record. She is the saint of purity, young women, victims of sexual assault, and *forgiveness.*

Born into a farming family of seven children in 1890, Maria's family suffered hardships after her father passed away some nine years later, prompting Maria's family to share a home with another family. One afternoon when she was eleven, Alessandro Serenelli, the twenty-year-old son of the family Maria lived with, made sexual advances to her. When Maria refused to submit, she was stabbed fourteen times. Although taken to the hospital, Maria died, but not before professing her forgiveness for her assailant. Although Alessandro was unrepentant for many years, he had a vision in jail that Maria appeared to him, gathering then offering him white lilies. In his vision, upon acceptance of the lilies, each one turned into a white flame. This experience profoundly changed Alessandro. After twenty-seven years of serving his sentence, Alessandro begged Maria's mother for her forgiveness, which she granted. Later, and for the rest of his life, Alessandro became a lay brother and gardener in a Capuchin monastery.

St. Maria's story is an inspiring story of faith, grace, mercy, love, and forgiveness. Her story is important to note because of the forgiveness she extended in life—*and death*—and the miracle it produced in Alessandro's life. Indeed, exploring forgiveness can afford everyone tremendous healing and peace.

In *Under the Tropical Skies*, I also wanted to delve into how our family elders can offer valuable life experiences providing us with helpful information and food for thought to apply to our lives. I am forever grateful for my dear, loving, amazing paternal Grandparents (Leo and Mary Ridini) and my maternal Grandparents (Anna and William White and Leo and Teresa Murphy). They have impacted my life profoundly with their constant love and support.

I invite you to read the Kate Grace novels:

- *Lady in the Window* (2018 American Fiction Awards' *Visionary Award Winner*; Hawai'i Book Publishers Association Ka Palapala Po'okela Awards, *Aloha From*

Across the Sea Award Finalist, 2019; and 2017 *Best Book Awards Fiction: Romance Winner*);
- *The Paradise Table,* an *Amazon Bestseller*;
- *Secrets of Grace Manor,* also a bestseller.

Find out more at:

https://www.MaryannRidiniSpencer.com

And check out my Amazon Author Page by searching *Maryann Ridini Spencer* or navigating to this link:

https://www.amazon.com/Maryann-Ridini-Spencer/e/B06XBHH6YK

Aloha,

Maryann

The Heart of Forgiveness

by Maryann Ridini Spencer

They cut to the Core,
Thoughts, words, actions—mine, yours—
like daggers, they pierce the heart
leaving pieces …
Strewn about
this way and *that*.
We struggle to find meaning while we *bleed.*
The war in our heads, unrelenting as we try
to make sense of it all.
Time and prayers to Our Father above help the wounds.
Understanding and empathy are also our Guides.
It does no good to hold revenge in our hearts,
or hate on our lips,
Less it eats away at the body and soul bit by bit.
Rather, compassion and love be the noble way,
treating one another as we would want to be treated as
Our Lord doth say.

For my Grandparents

A Grandparent's Love

by Maryann Ridini Spencer

A Grandparent's love is like a blanket that securely enfolds, warming our bodies and hearts and penetrating our souls.

As we grow tended to with our elder's sage words of advice,
We learn values and lessons that serve us throughout our lives.

If, by God's grace, we are blessed with their presence as we mature,
We can realize, by example, the value of how their love unconditionally and ceaselessly endures.

A grandparent's love is like a blanket that securely binds, bonding us together forever, entwined.

Taormina, Province of Messina, Italy, 1868

"Annabella! *Mio Amore!*" Costanza Costa's singsong call summoning her daughter floats up on the tail of a refreshing ocean breeze to the third-floor garden terrace at Villa Maria, a charming, elegant nineteenth-century, thirty-room stone villa perched high above the ocean floor and tucked into the jagged hillside above Taormina, Italy.

"*Un minuto*, Mamma!" replies Annabella as she caresses her painter's canvas with her brush and a perfect shade of crystal blue, capturing the transparent, azure Ionian Sea waters surrounding the villa.

The balmy breeze continues to roll up from the ocean below as Annabella backs away from her masterful watercolor. Still holding her paintbrush, she uses the back of her hand to push aside several strands of her silky chestnut-colored hair that the wind has disengaged from her chignon comb.

"*Perfètto.*" She sighs as she views her work-in-progress from several angles. Annabella's painting captures a stunning view of Villa Maria's terraced garden flora. Lush crimson bougainvillea explodes next to swaying palms. White plumeria blossoms, their golden centers and abundant pink roses in full bloom, frame a bird's-eye view of the distant panoramic ocean vista, which, hugged by Taormina's rocky coastline, provides a magnificent, unobstructed view of the majestic Mt. Etna, Europe's most active volcano.

Desirous of adding more of the sky's sublime golden hue to the image, Annabella picks up another brush, dips the tip into a blend of amber color, and adds several strokes to the canvas to create the intended effect.

"*Sto arrivando.* I'm putting my paints away," Annabella calls out once more to her mother. "I'm on my way." Then, just as she begins to head toward her chambers to dress for the evening's soiree, the family's annual summer dinner ball, Annabella becomes transfixed as the sky transmutes into a sublime yellow-magenta hue, forming a streak of garnet through the horizon's overlapping center.

Watching this glorious dance of color in the sky, Annabella sighs. Suddenly, the tactile shift in the surrounding atmosphere becomes palpable. She is acutely aware of her environment and has the empathy to tap into the unseen and unspoken. The kinetic energy that embraces her lifts her spirits to such a level that, although she does not know consciously in the present why she feels as she does, she knows from experience that the reason will unfold. What she does sense in the air is akin to … *magic*.

"*For it was not into my ear you whispered, but into my heart. It was not my lips you kissed, but my soul.*"

~~Judy Garland

1

Taormina, Province of Messina, Italy, 1868

The dreamy sounds of violin, piano, and flute blend harmoniously as Annabella makes her way into Villa Maria's stately ballroom. Tonight will be a gathering of friends, family, and many of her father's business associates in the family's import-export shipping empire. Annabella scans the room for familiar faces among the guests scattered about the room as a rush of warm wind caresses her bare shoulders.

Men wearing black coats and tails with white waistcoats, cravats, and fashionable, well-fitting pantaloons laugh and chat with lady guests in the glow of the oil lamps, moonlight, and firelight emanating from several massive, wood-burning stone fireplaces. Strategically placed oil lamps also lend a festive glow. The women guests, their hair beset with ribbons, flowers, and gilded combs, wear crinoline gowns made in an array of colorful hues. Their frocks, cut from delicate satin, silk, and lace fabrics, showcase decorative plunging necklines, fitted bodices, and off-the-shoulder sleeves. Annabella can't help but think the women resemble bell-shaped garden flowers in bloom.

During lulls in the music, the muffled sounds of voices and frantic movement of Villa Maria's extensive staff are heard as they tend to last-minute details in the dining room behind the large sets of carved-wood double doors.

Stefano Bianchi, a handsome twenty-three-year-old with a pleasant demeanor, approaches Annabella from behind and takes her by surprise, planting a kiss on the back of her exposed neck. "You are more breathtaking than tonight's evening sky," he whispers.

Dressed in an exquisite pale pink, off-the-shoulder gown with an embroidered corset adorned with floral lace appliques, a design that carries through onto the tulle skirt, Annabella is truly a vision. Her long silky hair is pulled up off her neck in a delicate, weaved pattern embellished with her favorite flowers—plumerias—and silver combs laden with pearls.

"And you smell good, too." Stefano sniffs the air filled with the intoxicating aroma of plumeria from Annabella's hair.

"Behave now," playfully scolds Annabella.

Since childhood, and only three years older than Annabella, Stefano delights in making Annabella laugh and watches over her with a keen, protective eye. Yet, beneath his playful façade and sometimes brotherly way, Stefano loves Annabella and hopes to make her his wife someday.

While attracted to Stefano's handsome visage, Annabella, not unaware of Stefano's intensified romantic feelings toward her, chooses to keep emotions at bay, preferring to enjoy her youth in the comfort of her parents' doting care for just a bit longer. "Have you seen my parents?" Annabella's eyes dart around the ballroom.

"Over there." Stefano motions. "They greeted me when I arrived."

"Let me say hello to them, and afterward, perhaps meet you in the refreshment room in ten minutes or so before the dancing commences?"

"I'll be waiting." Stefano, playful, winks as he takes Annabella's hand and kisses it.

Costanza Costa, Annabella's mother, a beautiful, olive-skinned, raven-haired woman with an impeccable figure, is dressed in a cream-colored floral tulle and lace gown. She stands next to her husband, Antonio, a handsome, elegant man with a head of salt-and-pepper hair, dark brown eyes, and an impeccably manicured mustache.

"*Bella, mi acara,*" praises Antonio as he touches Annabella's cheek. "You are a vision tonight."

Costanza hugs her daughter. "Bella, you look lovely, my darling. For a moment earlier this evening, I was sincerely worried that I might not be able to tear you away from your painting."

The love Annabella feels for her parents is all-encompassing. She is blessed, and she knows it. The Costas live well, and the family's successful agricultural import-export business, founded by Anabella's paternal grandfather, has flourished under her father's doting care and keen business acumen. Costanza, always her husband's champion and the perfect hostess, has also been an asset to the family business, which has served the family empire well. Costanza and Antonio grew up in the same circles together. While Antonio's family excelled in the import-export shipping arena, Costanza's family were wealthy bankers. So their families, lifelong friends, were thrilled when, at age twenty, Antonio proposed to Costanza, age eighteen. Devoted to one another and happily in love for twenty-two years and counting, Costanza and Antonio serve as perfect role models for a happy marriage. And Annabella, their only child, is their pride and joy.

After exchanging pleasantries with the crowd of well-wishers hugging both her parents, Annabella quickly makes a beeline to meet Stephano in the refreshment room.

"*Scusami!*" gushes Annabella with embarrassment as she crashes into a dashing gentleman.

Instead of being upset, the man flashes a devastatingly perfect smile. Standing over six feet tall, with an impressive physique, dark silky hair, chiseled features, and piercing blue eyes, Annabella can't help but think this is the most gorgeous man she has ever seen, even though he appears to be several years her senior.

Feeling as if she just found herself teetering on the edge of one of Taormina's jagged cliffs, Annabella feels her face burn. She takes a deep breath to anchor herself. The handsome man appears oblivious to her instant and utter inner turmoil.

"Giovanni!" Annabella's father suddenly embraces the man who holds Annabella's startled gaze. "May I introduce my daughter, Annabella. Annabella, Signor Giovanni Ricci."

"Delighted," Giovanni says with a smile. "May I?" He reaches for Annabella's hand as she extends her arm. Annabella takes a quick breath when she feels the tender warmth of Giovanni's electric kiss as the current courses through her gloved hand then throughout her body. Surprised by the unexpected feelings he has ignited, she wonders, *Why do I feel like I've met him before?*

Shaken back to reality from her déjà vu as a group of her father's business associates clamor around Antonio and Giovanni, Annabella tries to make sense of her visceral reaction to Signor Ricci as she flees to the familiar safety of Stephano.

Months after her parents' ball, Annabella still can't seem to shake the image of Giovanni's smile from her mind's eye. He has also infiltrated her dreams. The very thought and feelings conjured remembering the warmth of his kiss on her gloved hand at her parents' ball create such an explosive reflex throughout her being that she has to breathe deeply for several minutes to calm her constitution. More than anything, she wonders why she feels this way and ponders the possible meanings.

Why do I feel as if we have met? How could that be when we have not?

Annabella prays for clarity and understanding, but no answer is forthcoming.

"Annabella, *mio caro*, we'll be dining today at one o'clock," Costanza informs Annabella one Sunday morning.

Annabella and her parents customarily dine at Annabella's maternal grandparents' estate, Villa Romano, each week following Sunday mass. The afternoon meal, which generally consists of several courses—soup and salad, pasta, fish or meat, and various vegetables—is followed by a delectable dessert, usually at the home of Annabella's paternal grandparents. This way, both sets of grandparents share the day with their beloveds. However, today, dinner will take place at Villa Maria.

"A few of your father's business associates will be joining us for dessert," continues Costanza. "So please don't change your dress. It's lovely on you, and you must look your best for our guests."

"Yes, Mamma. I'll be on the terrace garden until then."

"Painting?"

"Don't worry." Annabella chuckles. "I'll wear a robe!"

For the next few hours, Annabella sketches a still life, a colorful serving bowl filled with yellow peaches, ruby-colored prickly pears, green and deep-purple grapes, and juicy, ripe, blood oranges.

"Signorina, the guests have arrived," announces Flora, Annabella's plump, happy-faced lady's maid, as she steps through the wooden doors leading out onto the garden terrace from Annabella's chambers. Flora, having helped raise Annabella since infancy, is like family.

Annabella puts a few last-minute touches to her painting.

"Come, sweetheart, we need to fix your hair," urges Flora. "The ocean winds have created quite a disturbance."

Annabella joins her parents at the dinner table set with the family's finest crystal, china, linens, and wines. This afternoon, Costanza's parents Ricardo and Lucia, and her mother's sister, Caterina, and Caterina's husband, Michele, are also in attendance. Several of Antonio's business associates have also been invited to join the family for dessert.

This Sunday meal is one of Annabella's favorites—an antipasto comprised of cheeses, olives, and roasted peppers— followed by a first course of Pappardelle noodles mixed with heavy cream, fresh lemon juice and rind, and grated Parmesan cheese. The second course, a delicious branzino, a mild white fish roasted with olive oil and herbs, is served with a platter of fresh garden vegetables.

Immediately following dinner, the family moves from the formal dining room onto the terrace. They sit under a lattice pergola, overflowing with a roof of fiery red bougainvillea, to admire unobstructed views of the surrounding ocean and the setting sun. Carlo, the butler, serves limoncello cordials in petite, stemmed, crystal glassware. Meanwhile, Annabella strolls the adjacent gardens with her grandmother Lucia, who loves to take long walks after every meal, believing that walking aids in her body's digestion.

"Nonna," begins Annabella, taking her grandmother's hand. "Come, I want to show you how the plumeria bursts with new blossoms."

"*Bellissima!*" Lucia claps her hands as she stands before the abundant, sweet-smelling beauties. Annabella picks up one of the white jewels with its golden center and hands it to her grandmother, who inhales the perfume and moans with pleasure.

"It's the best fragrance in the world, isn't it?" Annabella laughs as she plucks a blossom for herself to appreciate as grandmother and granddaughter continue their stroll.

"*Ciao, Ciao!*"

Annabella hears a robust masculine voice happily greet her family as she and her grandmother return to the terrace.

"Papa, I want dessert!" singsongs an adorable little boy, who looks to be about seven, as he skips onto the terrace and grabs hold of his father's pant leg. "What are we having? Where is it?" The adults chuckle at the boy's enthusiasm.

"*Ciao*, my sweet Lorenzo." Costanzo gets up to embrace the little one.

The boy's father has his back turned away from Annabella. However, when he turns around to face her, Annabella draws a breath. *Giovanni!*

A staid-looking woman is ushered onto the terrace in a wheelchair, pushed by a nurse in a formal uniform. Annabella soon learns that the woman in the wheelchair is Giovanni's wife, Regina.

"Do you like cannoli?" Antonio asks Lorenzo, already knowing what the boy's answer will be.

"*Sì!*" Lorenzo runs to Antonio.

"But I don't think you like *gelato*. Correct?"

"*Nò!* I like gelato." Lorenzo bobs his head up and down enthusiastically to emphasize his answer.

Servers pass a tray of cannoli overflowing with ricotta cheese filling and another platter, decorated with a selection of citrus sorbets, around the table previously set with plates, napkins, and silverware. A large platter with a mélange of dried fruits and nuts is also placed at the center of the table while Carlo takes orders for expressos and more limoncello liqueurs.

"Regina suffered a spinal cord injury after a fall from a horse several years ago," whispers Lucia to Annabella during dessert.

The damage, no doubt, thinks Annabella, probably has much to do with Regina's sour demeanor. Regina continually snaps at her husband and son during the visit and rarely offers a smile or uplifting remark. In addition to her outlook, Regina's injury must have also affected her appearance. Although attractive, she looks worn, tired, and years older than her vibrant husband.

Lorenzo, a highly inquisitive, happy child full of energy, sits next to Anabella. The charming boy wastes no time sharing with her how he loves to read, listen to music, and play with his friend Paolo. Annabella can't help but notice that the child, with his head of black hair, handsome features, deep blue eyes, and charming smile, makes him the spitting image of his father.

When Lorenzo barrages Annabella with questions about the flowers in the garden, Antonio suggests his daughter take the boy on a tour.

"Can my father come too?" asks Lorenzo.

"Of course." Annabella nods. She smiles at Giovanni. "And Signora Costa, would you like to accompany us?"

"*Nò*. I prefer to stay here. *Grazie*," answers Regina.

Lorenzo takes both Annabella's and Giovanni's hand as they stroll through the terrace gardens. Annabella points out several varieties of palm trees, the orange, pink, purple and red shades of the bougainvillea, the sweet-smelling orange and lemon trees, her mother's prized roses, several varieties of jasmine, and the white, yellow, and pink plumerias.

Lorenzo takes deep inhalations of the sweet-smelling plumerias. "These are my favorite."

"Mine too." Annabella smiles.

"This lovely tour makes me feel like we're taking a little vacation," marvels Giovanni. The terraced gardens, which showcase several unique seating areas, viewpoints, and stone water fountains, features beautifully carved wooden benches and doors leading to other floral paths.

When Giovanni flashes his beautiful smile again, Annabella feels her knees start to buckle. Lorenzo breaks the spell when he picks up a fallen rose, the blossom still intact, and hands it to Annabella.

"I think he likes you," whispers Giovanni. The comment makes Annabella's face flush.

"Who's painting this?" asks Lorenzo as he heads toward an artist's easel and the bowl of fruit Annabella used earlier that morning as her still life inspiration.

"Me. Would you like to see some of my work?" asks Annabella.

"Yes!" Lorenzo is emphatic.

"*Prego*." Annabella ushers Giovanni and Lorenzo into her gallery, just off the terrace.

"Your paintings are beautiful," marvels Giovanni gazing at Annabella's canvases showcasing exquisite landscapes, cobblestone streets, outdoor cafes, and piazzas in Florence and Rome. Others feature Tuscan vineyards, green hills, and valleys adorned with golden light, panoramic views of the Sicilian coast, the markets in Taormina, and a range of still-life works. "Lorenzo loves art. He's always telling me he wants to learn how to paint," says Giovanni. "Lorenzo, what do you think of Annabella's paintings?"

"I love them! Annabella, will you teach me to paint?"

"I've never taught anyone but myself," Annabella replies, amused at the little boy's enthusiasm.

"*Per favore*?" implores Lorenzo, making Annabella's heart melt.

Annabella looks at Giovanni for his suggestion.

"If you're willing, we would appreciate it."

"Okay then," Annabella accepts. "When would you like to begin?"

"We'll check with my wife, but perhaps Saturdays after Lorenzo's piano lessons."

"*Grazie!*" Lorenzo dances about, clapping joyfully.

Later that evening, after the guests have retired for home and her parents to their bed chamber, Annabella sits alone out on her bedroom terrace. The glow of the moon and the twinkling stars in the dark evening sky paint a shimmery blanket over the calm ocean waters.

"Thank you, Lord, for my many blessings—my parents, grandparents, all my family and friends, and for Stefano," prays Annabella.

As Annabella ponders the afternoon—the delicious Sunday meal, walking with her beloved nonna in the garden, dessert with the Riccis, showing the adorable Lorenzo and his handsome father her paintings—she is filled with peace, love, and gratitude. She can also hardly believe she'll be teaching Lorenzo how to paint. Already, the precocious boy has won her heart.

Thinking more about her feelings, although Giovanni's smile might make her heart stop, she respects the fact that he is married, not to mention one of her father's business associates, and quickly puts any thoughts of him out of her mind.

Her dreams, however, are another matter.

Over the next few evenings, while she sleeps, Giovanni makes surprise cameo appearances. His smile, laughter, calm demeanor, and gentle touch holding her arm as they walk through the garden remain with Annabella in waking hours. Although no words are spoken in her dreams, Annabella can't shake the fulfillment she feels in her heart when Giovanni is near—and she senses Giovanni feels the same.

After every such dream, upon waking, Annabella reminds herself, *Such love cannot and will never be.*

Today, like the other mornings of late, she admonishes herself for such fantastical nonsense, submerges any romantic thoughts, and begins her day.

"Be present in all things and thankful for all things."

~~Maya Angelou

2

Hanalei, Kauai—Present Day

"Aloha, my lovely," Kai Stevens greets his pretty wife, Kate, as he steps out onto their massive lanai which overlooks their beautiful, well-tended gardens situated steps away from Kauai's majestic Hanalei Bay. He plants a wet kiss on Kate's lips before he sits down for breakfast.

"Another, please," moans Kate, enticing Kai, who happily obliges. "You always look so handsome in your blue hospital scrubs."

Originally hailing from Long Island's Gold Coast, Kate, a lifestyle journalist and novelist, met Kai during a business trip to Kauai. On that fateful trip, Kate interviewed her now dear BFF, Olivia Larkin, a well-known TV talk-show host, magazine publisher, and business entrepreneur. Afterward, Olivia invited Kate to a small dinner gathering at her Princeville home. Upon meeting Kai, an ER doctor with a pleasant demeanor, sparks began to fly between Kate and Kai. However, it wasn't until Kate's second, extended trip to the Garden Isle that the young lovers formed a romantic bond. Weeks later, after becoming engaged, Kate realized she could work on assignments remotely with her *New York View* magazine publisher. With Kai being well established in his post at the local hospital, the couple, who share a mutual love and affinity for living The Way of Aloha, felt choosing Kauai as their home was an obvious choice.

"Yum." Kai licks the sweet pineapple juice off his fingers after popping a wedge of Sugarloaf into his mouth.

"This one is exceptionally delicious," agrees Kate as she picks up another wedge from the plate of pineapple and pops the juicy tidbit into her mouth.

"Ready for the main event?" asks Kate, lifting the cover from a serving plate to reveal a steaming mix of curried tofu, last night's grilled vegetables—a selection of asparagus tips, sliced mushrooms, and taro, a root vegetable with a nutty taste—tossed together with sweet potato, diced Maui onion, and sautéed kale.

"Pile it on." Kai holds up his plate, and Kate doles out a generous portion. "I love when you make this leftover scramble. Glad you put in the kale, too."

"We have so much in our garden. I should take some over to your sister. I'm sure The Plumeria Café could use it."

Kai nods. "Malie would love that. She'll also want to sell it at the café's market."

"Excellent idea. I'll tell my dad to pick a few baskets before heading over there this morning."

"Have him pick some tomatoes and zucchini, too. We'll never be able to eat all we've planted."

Kai's younger, married sister, Malie Kapule, co-owns The Plumeria Café, a popular local eatery in the heart of Hanalei, with Olivia Larkin. The café recently took over the shop next door, turning it into a grocery market and gift shop managed by Kate's father, Glen, Glen's lady friend, Jessie, and Kai's father, Bradford.

Kate nods in agreement, knowing her father would love to take some of the garden produce he's helped to shepherd along.

After his beloved wife Catherine's passing, Kate's father makes his winter home in Kai and Kate's *ohana* (guesthouse). In the summer, to be near his other children, Kate's elder siblings, Carla and Derek, and their families, Glen lives in a newly purchased townhome in a quaint waterfront village on Long Island's North Shore. Glen, Jessie, and Bradford, who all not too long ago suffered the loss of their beloved spouses, have not only all become friends but have all found extraordinary healing and new life in magical Hanalei.

Kate often reminisces how her life changed after her first trip to Kauai when she met and interviewed Olivia. After the trip, upon returning home she experienced an avalanche of heartbreak—splitting with her supposed "soulmate" Jason and the quick passing of her mother from a brain tumor. When Olivia saw her friend in an apparent state of depression, she invited Kate, as her guest, to return to Kauai for a chance to relax and regroup. On that second trip, Kate and Kai bonded. Eternally grateful, Kate thanks the Creator daily for this blessing and the new trajectory of her life.

Kate's creativity has flourished living in the land of Aloha— she writes her novels and works on her freelance magazine assignments for the magazines, *New York View* and *Olivia!,* and her online magazine site, *gardenofaloha.com.* She also develops recipes and even manages to sell and create merchandise for The Plumeria Café and The Plumeria Market.

"What time will you be home tonight, sweet?" Kate tops off her coffee mug with more of the rich Kona brew kept hot in a stainless-steel, insulated carafe.

"Late again."

Kate makes a sad face.

"I know, babe. I might even have to pull a double. Jiro sent me a text saying he might be unable to make it. Since he covered for me when we went to Europe—"

"Okay. I'll see if I can hang with one of my Nā Pīkake sisters. Kate demonstrates the Hawaiian shaka sign for "hang loose," waving her right thumb and pinkie in the air with the middle fingers curled under her palm. Kate and some of her friends—Olivia, Jessie, Malie, Malie's sister-in-law, Alana Kapule, a Hanalei police officer, realtor friend Elaine Harrison, and Sukey Tadashi, co-owner with her husband, Kamal, of The Princeville Art Gallery—formed the group Nā Pīkake. At first just a social club, Nā Pīkake blossomed into an organization that works with local nonprofits supporting various worthy causes.

"I'll give you a ring later. Aloha." Kai and Kate kiss once more before he pulls out of the driveway onto Weke Road.

"The balmy breeze is so divine," purrs Kate as a gust of warm wind tousles her hair. She tucks the wild strands behind both ears as she sits on her friend Olivia's backyard lanai with Kai's sister, Malie.

"Can I get you ladies anything more to eat or drink?" asks Olivia, heading back to her kitchen through the open, floor-to-ceiling, accordion glass doors.

"Not for me," calls Malie. She's nursing her cappuccino and watching as the sun dips into the calm ocean in a multi-colored spectacle. "I can't eat another bite. Dinner was delicious." She sits next to Kate on a comfortable, overstuffed sofa decorated in a colorful tropical pattern.

"Kate?"

"I'm good," answers Kate, pulling out her iPhone to snap a few photos of the gorgeous sunset.

Olivia's cell phone rings as she returns to the lanai, and she reads the incoming text. "We're on for this weekend, Malie," she confirms. "Jessie just sent me a text saying she and Kate's dad will man The Plumeria Café while we're in Kona.

"Kona?" cries Kate. "You didn't tell me you were going to Kona!"

"Olivia and I are giving ourselves a much-needed break from the café." Malie says in a matter-of-fact tone of voice.

"NOT!" Olivia makes the sound of a gong. "Malie's pulling your leg."

Who, me? Never." Malie chuckles. "This is a girls' *work* weekend. And—"

"I wasn't invited?" whines Kate.

"You're always invited," says Olivia. "But wouldn't you rather be home with Kai?"

"Well, as it so happens, Kai phoned me just before I got here tonight. He's working all weekend, filling in for a doctor with a family issue. So—"

"Fab, so you can join us!" Olivia claps her hands.

"Kidding aside, Olivia's checking out some new venues to film some TV segments of her show, and we also want to check out some new restaurants that are getting a lot of write-ups lately," Malie explains.

"Eating our way through the Kohala Coast—now that's going to be fun!" Olivia can't repress a huge grin.

"Hey, I bet I could dig up some fun stories for the magazine," Kate offers.

"Brilliant. Perfect," agrees Olivia. "It will be a win-win all the way around."

"What's going on? Are you okay, hon?" asks Kai later that evening, concerned when he hears Kate groan, accompanied by banging sounds coming from the master bathroom. A few moments later, Kate, sullen, exits the bathroom and crawls under the covers next to Kai.

"I've got my period."

"Okay." Kai scoops her into his arms and strokes Kate's hair.

"So we'll continue to try."

"Uh, that's kind of hard with your relentless work schedule," Kate responds in a flippant manner not customary to her usual demeanor. "I'm sorry," she says, immediately apologetic for her sour attitude.

"Sweetheart, please, don't worry. We've only just started to try. It'll happen."

"From your mouth to God's ears."

"It is in God's hands." Kai turns off the light on the night table next to them. "Come here," he whispers, pulling Kate in closer and kissing her tenderly. Then, finding comfort in each other's arms, they drift quickly asleep.

The following morning after Kai has left for the hospital, Kate finishes the last of her fresh brew, rinses out her coffee mug, and plops it into the dish rack next to the kitchen sink. Her usual morning ritual—coffee, getting dressed for her morning workout, breakfast, and a walk in the garden—is typically a calming and centering routine. However, in the last few weeks, instead of enjoying the delicious aroma and taste of her coffee, and the luscious sweetness of a bowl of freshly cut pineapple and berries mixed with Greek yogurt, all Kate can do is obsesses about becoming pregnant.

I've got to stop driving myself crazy. It will happen. She remembers the words Kai whispered to her last night. *It's in God's hands.*

Kate heads toward the backyard garden. Walking among the lush, ruby-red hibiscus, the sweet-smelling pikake bushes, she admires a perfectly formed plumeria blossom on the ground, picks it up and, bringing it to her nose, breathes deeply.

"Thank you, God, for our beautiful garden and all the amazing colors and scents." Kate whispers. "I want to let you know how grateful I am for my family, Kai, his family, and our friends—my ohana. I also want to thank you for my writing ability, health, and so many things. You know our hearts, my heart. If it is part of your plan, and I so pray it is, Kai and I would love to have a child to share our life. Help me to be strong and trust in your will. I love you, Father."

Kate continues to walk the garden, feeling more peaceful now that she's prayed. Later, she returns to the cottage to pack for her Kona weekend with Olivia and Malie.

"Friend time feeds the heart, body, mind, and soul."

~~Maryann Ridini Spencer

3

———

The Big Island of Hawaii, Present Day

"You'll love the private home where we're staying, ladies," trills Olivia in a singsong fashion as she leans her head back on the plush leather seat of the limousine. Olivia, Kate, and Malie, having just landed at the Big Island of Hawaii's Kona International Airport, are headed to their destination in Hualalai. "It's situated on a private beach between other estates and a five-star resort."

"I can't wait," admits Kate. She is happily taking in the views outside the limousine's window, where craggy black lava rocks are perched against pristine blue waters and breathtaking ocean vistas.

"Get your camera ready, Kate," instructs Malie. "So many gorgeous views to memorialize." The landscape becomes greener and lusher as they travel closer to their weekend home. Majestic palms and Monkeypod trees stand tall.

"You got that right!" Kate nods as she raises her iPhone just in time to capture the magnificent cascading blossoms of the rainbow shower trees as the limo drives the picturesque highway to their destination on Kaupulehu Drive.

"The sunrises and sunsets are spectacular," Olivia chimes in. "A different show every time."

"What's on the agenda once we unpack?" asks Kate.

"A trip to the local farmer's market followed by some R and R at the home's infinity pool," Olivia replies.

"And this evening, we'll be dining at The Paradise—the new five-star oceanfront eatery on Ali'i Drive, followed by a nightcap on our ocean-view lanai," enthuses Malie.

"Woo-hoo," cheers Kate as she takes more photos.

Moments later, the limo pulls up to a massive lava-rock wall with a driveway entrance consisting of an impressive wooden gate carved with tropical flora. When the driver opens his window and pushes several keys on the gate's keypad, a buzzer sounds as the gate opens.

Large Poinciana trees with umbrellas of crimson blossoms sit on either side of the winding paved road leading to a spectacular, modern home with clean lines and large, floor-to-ceiling windows that take in the exquisite lush garden and surrounding ocean views.

"Wow," Kate murmurs softly as she takes in the beauty.

"I know, right?" Olivia replies with a nod.

"How did you find this place?" inquires Malie.

"Our Nā Pīkake sister, real estate maven Elaine. How else?" Olivia chuckles. "If I didn't go through her, she'd never forgive me."

"She's definitely on top of her game." Now it's Malie who's pulling out her iPhone. "I'm going to tease Aukai and tell him how much his wife misses him. NOT!" Malie cackles playfully and snaps a few photos of the stunning home.

The estate butler, Uli, dressed in long white linen pants and a Hawaiian shirt, greets the ladies at the front entrance. He places a gorgeous orchid lei around each of their necks while the housekeeper, Lilo, dressed in an attractive, knee-length floral shirt dress and crisp white apron, shows the limo driver where to place the women's suitcases.

"Follow me, please," instructs Uli.

On either side of the open, lightly colored tile entryway, tall white walls lead to a gorgeous cathedral ceiling made of wood finished to reveal its natural patina. A wall of windows off the great room in the distance showcases a massive covered lanai, which beckons the guests to an infinity pool and priceless ocean and mountain views. The entire home is decorated in large, comfortably elegant, oversized white furniture complimented with natural wood flooring and exotic, custom-made accent pieces.

Adjacent to the great room, the kitchen continues with the same color scheme and ocean and mountain views. The dream kitchen is outfitted with chef-grade Thermador kitchen appliances and state-of-the-art designer fixtures. Six chairs surround a large quartz center island housing a gas cooktop and plenty of dining space under the contemporary pendant lighting designed with tropical flair.

"I think I'm in heaven," Kate declares.

"You and me both," agrees Malie, who, like Kate, also loves to cook and putter around the kitchen.

"I'll leave this room to you ladies." Olivia chuckles. "I know my limitations. Although, surprise, surprise, the housekeeper, Lilo, is also the chef. So I don't know how much time you'll spend in this room either."

After an outside tour, the ladies are shown to their suites, each with its own walk-in wardrobe, sitting room with desk, and sliders to a patio lanai with water views. Even their en suite bathrooms showcase ocean and mountain vistas.

Kate unpacks, freshens up from traveling, and texts Kai some sweet words, accompanied by a few impressive photos of the estate grounds, before heading out to the farmer's market.

Kai texts Kate back:

Have a great time, babe. The ER is extremely busy, so I'm glad you caught me on a quick break. Miss you so much, love you. I'll ring you later tonight. I want to hear about your day. XO.

Feeling energized and happy now that she's connected with her love, Kate's ready to enjoy a fun day.

Exploring the farmer's market in the heart of Kailua-Kona, the ladies find lots of freshly baked goods, abundant local produce, and plentiful displays of arts and crafts. Kate has a blast as she talks to the local farmers about what's in season, farming practices, and recipe ideas. She jots down names and numbers for potential *Olivia!* magazine articles and her gardenofaloha.com website. Attending the market also conjures up memories of her wonderful honeymoon experiences with Kai on the Big Island.

"I recognize the folks in that smoothie booth!" exclaims Kate. "They have the best flavors. Come on, ladies, I'll treat you!"

Soon, Kate, Olivia, and Malie are sitting under the shade of a covered lanai, sipping pineapple-coconut-mango shakes. After taking another sip of smoothie, Kate breaks off the top of a large, cakey, lemon-coconut-blueberry muffin the ladies also purchased to share. "Mmm. Delicious." Kate passes the muffin to Olivia, then Malie.

"Fantastic taste. Moist and just the right sweetness," notes Malie after sampling. "Do you think the muffin lady you purchased this from might want to share her recipe?"

"Already got it. Before sharing, I want to play around with the ingredients to eliminate the refined sugar."

"Thinking of using pureed fruit like you usually do?" asks Malie.

Kate nods." I just have to figure out what works best, taste-and consistency-wise."

"I just had a lightbulb moment!" Olivia's eyes widen. "I think we should do some location pieces around the island when we film the *Olivia!* TV show. The estate where we're staying can be our backdrop and home base. We shoot segments, like here, for example, where we talk to residents about the unique local arts and crafts, their farm-to-table produce—"

"And their recipe suggestions," Kate interjects.

Olivia nods and adds, "We'll do some cooking segments, too. Then, Kate, you could run with ideas for the magazine and your blog site."

"I've already been collecting names and numbers," says Kate.

"Great minds—" Malie comments with a wink.

Moments later, a little girl, about three years old, cries out. The dark-haired cutie with long, wavy hair and a pretty sundress stands by herself—no adult belonging to her in view. Kate's motherly instincts activate, and she makes a beeline to the girl.

"Sweetheart. What's the matter?"

The little girl sniffles, wiping tears from her cheek. "I lost my mommy."

"Oh, dear. My name's Kate. What's yours?"

"Makana."

"What a pretty name."

Olivia and Malie approach.

"The poor dear lost her mommy," explains Kate while the little girl continues to whimper.

"Let me find the market management table," Malie offers. "Perhaps they can make an announcement. You both stay here." Malie quickly departs, a woman on a mission.

Some fifteen minutes later, Malie brings back the little girl's mother.

"Mahalo. I'm Makana's mom, Kalea. The young, pretty, thirty-something thanks Kate, Malie, and Olivia as the little girl runs into her mommy's arms. "I've been frantic. I told Makana to stay in the tent, playing with her dolls. I'm filling in for my sister today. It's her booth.

She had an appointment for a few hours, so I said I'd cover for her."

"I'm sorry, Mommy," whispers Makana.

"Stay where I tell you from now on, okay? Then you won't get lost."

"Okay," replies the girl sweetly.

"It was nice to meet you." Kate smiles at Makana, who then throws her arms around Kate in a bear hug, melting Kate's heart.

"Come to our booth, Aloha Creations. It's close to the market entrance." Kalea points to the location in the distance. "I'd like to give you ladies a little something to show my appreciation."

The three walk with Kalea to the booth filled with beautiful one-of-a-kind pieces of jewelry and other items.

"This isn't necessary," Kate protests as Kalea fastens the clasp on a long silver chain around Kate's neck. From the chain hangs a pretty, hand-painted porcelain art piece displaying a beautiful spray of white lilies on a bed of green leaves.

Olivia and Malie are already wearing their custom necklaces—Olivia, a grouping of fiery red heliconia plants, and Malie, a garden of yellow-orange fiesta hibiscus.

"Look." Kalea turns Kate toward the booth's long mirror.

"It's gorgeous. Mahalo," Kate admits after admiring her gift in the mirror.

The ladies peruse the other beautiful creations in the booth, and Kate insists on purchasing a tabletop photo of gorgeous tropical flowers and their meanings. Olivia and Malie decide on oversized totes crafted from colorful, tropically-patterned material.

"Bye, bye!" Makana waves, after which she blows some kisses to the ladies as the three leave the booth, and they respond in kind.

"She's just so adorable," gushes Kate, wiping a tear from her eye. Quite emotional now, Kate fights to hold back more tears.

"Hey, girlfriend. Are you okay?" asks Olivia while Malie looks on, concerned.

Kate sighs deeply to anchor herself. "Yeah. Oh. Wow. Where did that come from?"

"You're such a softy." Malie smiles to make light of Kate's distress and elicits a laugh from Kate.

"I'll explain what I think might be going on when we get in the car," Kate promises, and the three head toward their rented, black Land Rover.

"So." Olivia pulls away from the curb and wastes no time finding out what Kate wishes to share. In the middle row, Malie leans into Kate, who's sitting in the passenger seat.

"I'll let you guys in on a little secret since you caught me in a weak moment," begins Kate. "Pinky swear it's just between us and no one else." Kate takes turns clasping pinky fingers with Malie then Olivia. "My outburst of tears today is probably due to me PMSing, but the truth is, Kai and I have been trying to get pregnant."

The car erupts into joyous screams from Olivia and Malie.

"I know, you guys. But I had my period again."

"How long have you been trying?" Olivia asks.

"Two months."

"Oh, Kate, that's not long at all." Malie rubs Kate's arm in a comforting gesture.

"That's what Kai says."

"Well, he's right," Olivia confirms emphatically.

"I guess helping that little girl ignited my mama instincts."

"It's okay. It's all going to be okay." Olivia pats Kate's shoulder.

The car is silent now. Noticing all the lush tropical beauty outside, Kate leans out her open window and inhales deeply. She relishes the warm caresses of the sun and the sublime, soothing breezes. Thanking the Creator for all the blessings she does have, including gems like Olivia, Malie, and all her Nā Pīkake sisters, a sense of calm, happiness, and well-being suddenly fills her senses.

The ladies' evening dining spot, The Paradise, lives up to its name. Situated on a multi-acre parcel of land by the shore's edge, the magnificent bamboo structure boasts indoor and outdoor seating with panoramic ocean views. The ladies dine in a private spot in the outdoor garden area lit by pretty hanging solar pendants. The soothing sound of waves crashing at the shoreline is the music that greets them before a slack key ensemble plays melodic instrumentals.

An attentive waiter serves their dinner—the first course of individual salads made with various greens, heirloom tomatoes, avocado, cucumber, and crispy Maui onion shavings mixed with a heavenly lilikoi dressing. Next, macadamia-encrusted mahi-mahi is served with a spicy peanut sauce and a medley of fresh vegetables and jasmine rice. Finally, the trio enjoys a round of decaf cappuccinos as they take their eager spoons to a traditional Hawaiian dessert—a massive piece of chocolate haupia pie, the thick custard center made from coconut milk and chocolate morsels topped with whipped cream.

At a table across from the ladies sits a young family of four—mother, father, a boy around twelve, and a daughter a few years younger. The children, dressed in their best, are very well behaved. Kate can't help but keep glancing over. At one point, she catches Olivia watching her and smiling, prompting Kate to remember Olivia's poignant experience with motherhood.

Not too long ago, Olivia shared her decades-held secret with Kate and then the world—she had been raped as a very young teen. Afterward, Olivia, who had just crossed the brink of womanhood, learned she was pregnant. Barely more than a child herself, she chose to put the baby girl up for adoption, a choice her grandparents, her guardians after her mother's passing, had also approved.

Taking Kate into her confidence, Olivia could face her demons, after which she found the strength to meet and forge a friendship with her now-grown child, Alia, a successful ER doctor living in Boston.

Abandoning her secret also allowed Olivia to navigate painful memories and associations related to the attack. Eventually, she could finally commit to and deepen her relationship with her longtime love, Grant Anderson, a successful real estate developer and an all-around great person.

"You're so lucky you have Alia, Olivia. Do you ever wish you had more children?" asks Kate before taking another sip of her cappuccino.

"Honestly, it might have been nice. However, I would have never had a child as a single parent. I was always the type to want to do that as a couple. Besides, I've had such a brilliant, fun career that I've kept myself quite busy. Back in the day, when I started my career, things were much different than they are for women today. As a single parent back then, I could have never done half the things I've managed." She turns to Malie and asks, "What about you, Malie?"

"I'd like two. God willing, a boy and a girl." Malie dips her fork into what's left of the haupia pie. "Aukai agrees. Maybe we'll start in the next year or two. With me only in my early thirties, we still have time."

"Tick-tock," clicks Olivia several times, making Malie and Kate laugh.

"That's a good number, Malie." Kate sips the remainder of her coffee. "God willing for me too."

"Well, I'm happy that my baby, Alia, is all grown," chirps Olivia. "She said she wants to come out for a vacay and time it to our next Nā Pīkake fundraiser."

"Which will be?" asks Malie.

"TBD and up for discussion at next month's meeting."

"'For I know the plans I have for you,'
declares the Lord, 'plans to prosper you and
not to harm you, plans to give you a hope
and a future.'"

~~Jeremiah 29:11

4

Hanalei, Kauai, Present Day

Back in Kauai after a successful trip scouting locations and story ideas for the *Olivia!* television show and magazine, Kate flips through the tabletop book of Hawaiian flowers that includes their meanings as well as anecdotal stories.

The lily ... a symbol of good luck. The flower is associated with purity, rebirth, fertility, and motherhood. In religious iconography, they often represent the Virgin Mary and are also often depicted at the Resurrection of Christ.

"Wow!" says Kate aloud. She examines the pendant around her neck and utters a little prayer. The Creator knows her desire.

"Kate! Can you help?" Kai is in the backyard, where he is stringing up another row of solar lights on the wooden pergola.

Kate comes to Kai's aid and holds up the string of lights so Kai can affix them to the pergola's wooden beams. "Lookin' good."

"Hopefully, the solar panels will charge so we can check our handiwork tonight."

Kate watches her husband as he moves. She can't believe how lucky she is. Not only is he gorgeous in his baseball cap, Bermuda shorts, and a fitted T-shirt that outlines his muscular physique, he is also loving and kind. Kate is certain Kai has no idea she is watching him so intently with these growing thoughts of desire in her mind.

Suddenly, Kai catches Kate's eye and shoots her one of his delicious smiles. Instinctively understanding her thoughts, he sets his tools down and walks to her. He places his arms around her waist and pulls her to his chest, looking soulfully into her eyes.

"You're so beautiful." Kai's fingers gently touch the exposed skin around Kate's neck and face, then travel to her exposed shoulders and the top of her back. He can feel her shiver as he teases her with little kisses along her neck. Then, slightly parting his mouth, his tongue gently brushes against her skin.

As Kai's hands caress Kate's sides and back, electric shocks ignite her being. "My love, you're making my knees weak," moans Kate, taking in his musky scent.

Kai, pleased with Kate's admission, pulls her even closer, and the warmth and heat become combustible. "Well, we have all afternoon to do something about that." After a deep, soul kiss, Kai picks up Kate and carries her inside the house.

A work-free weekend for Kate and Kai of loving, dining out on delicious food, snorkeling, and boating is literally what the doctor ordered. Walking hand in hand at the local monthly arts-and-crafts fair in Hanalei town, the couple chats up the artists and peruse the expert locally made wares. Townsfolk meander, and a live band play well-loved Hawaiian tunes while a shaved ice vendor delights patrons with his colorful, sugary treats.

"Aloha!" Sukey Tadashi, an attractive Japanese woman, one of Kate's Nā Pīkake sisters, and her Eurasian husband, Kamal, wave to Kate and Kai.

"Fancy meeting you here," says Kate, knowing it's exactly the type of venue where Sukey and Kamal would frequent. The ladies embrace.

"Looking out for more local talent," replies Sukey, who, along with Kamal, owns the Princeville Art Gallery on Kuhio Highway. "I'm surprised you're not exhibiting today, Kate."

"My photography is already on display at your gallery. That's good enough for me with all I have going on. Besides, Kai and I needed some alone time this weekend. He's been working so hard lately."

"Yeah," pouts Kai playfully. "Say, you guys want to grab a bite? We're on our way to The Plumeria Café.

"You're sure we aren't intruding?" Sukey winks at Kate.

"We'd love it if you would join us," Kate assures her.

The Plumeria Café is overflowing with its regulars in addition to the crowd attending the arts and crafts fair. "Do you think you might have some pull with the management?" asks Kamal, realizing the wait for a table could take a while.

"We called Malie to let her know we were coming. She's got a table waiting for us out on the lanai."

As they eat, the couples' gathering grows when they are joined by Olivia, Grant, Elaine, and Elaine's husband, Trevor.

"We should have made this a Nā Pīkake lunch with our other sisters and their men," states Olivia.

"Well, Alana is on call with the Hanalei police today, and her husband, Hani, couldn't make it," interjects Sukey.

"Malie's managing here, and Aukai's working with Jessie and my dad at the market," adds Kate. "So, it's just us."

"Here, here, then. I'll toast to us!" Trevor Harrington, a handsome, silver-haired, sophisticated man, holds his wine glass high.

"I'll drink to that," concurs Elaine. Trevor and Elaine are transplants from England to Kauai and speak with beautiful, distinctive British accents. "Speaking of Nā Pīkake, we agreed to have our monthly meetings Thursday nights starting next week, right?"

"Yes," confirms Olivia. "I'm hosting. Six p.m. Potluck."

"Well, daahling, I'll pick up something yummy," gushes Elaine. "My skills in the kitchen are—"

"Quite dangerous," Trevor interrupts with a chuckle. The table breaks out in laughter. Elaine is a confessed expert at take-out.

"That's descriptive of my talent in the kitchen, too," Olivia says as she and Elaine clink glasses.

"Daahling, we all can't be a Kate or Malie," quips Elaine, raising her eyebrows to emphasize. More laughter.

"While we have a forum here, any suggestions we can present to our Nā Pīkake sisters next week about fundraiser ideas?" asks Olivia.

As the table ponders the question, Kate finally breaks the silence. "How about families in need? A fundraiser where we might help not only raise money but offer support to foster family relationships, communication, understanding."

Olivia nods. " I like that. Families need assistance in so many ways."

"I have several health-care professionals as clients that I could wrangle up to help," offers Elaine.

"Same here," volunteers Kai.

"Kamal and I work with a few artists who do healing through the arts," Sukey chimes in.

"Fantastic. Let's write down all our ideas and contacts for next week's meeting," Kate instructs. "Send them to me, and I'll write them up for our meeting agenda and distribute it before we gather so the other Nā Pīkake sisters can think on it."

5

"You're perfectly healthy." Dr. Monica Yoshida, Kate's OB-GYN, fills in Kate on her latest lab tests several weeks after Kate's last period. Dr. Yoshida sits behind a massive wooden desk covered with work files and photographs of happy families and newborns.

"Good to know." Kate fidgets with the lily pendant around her neck.

"Relax, enjoy. It'll happen."

"That's what my husband says."

"Well, he's right."

Try not to obsess, thinks Kate as she climbs into the driver's seat of her silver Honda Accord Hybrid sedan. Feeling better after the positive report by Dr. Yoshida, Kate is filled with a renewed sense of well-being.

Driving back to Hanalei from Princeville and listening to the melodic, slack key guitar instrumentals on the local radio, Kate occasionally peers to her left at the mosaic patchwork of the taro fields off the Kuhio Highway. Then, traveling over the single-lane, historic, steel-truss Hanalei bridge, surrounded by lush green mountains to her left and the Pacific Ocean to her right, Kate feels transported. Her mind wanders back to the online Generations.com ancestry search she made of her father's lineage a year ago. She feels blessed that she solved the family mystery of what happened to a young child who went missing in eighteenth-century England.

What must it be like to have a child and then have it go missing?

Kate's thoughts turn to the importance of family—her mother, father, sister and brother, her nieces and nephew, grandparents and aunts, uncles, and cousins—and how very dear they are to her. She's incredibly grateful that she was born into such a loving family. Kate hopes she'll be able to build her special family unit with Kai to carry on for future generations.

Love and family. It's what it's all about.

Once home, Kate heads for the kitchen and pulls bags of fresh veggies—kale, broccolini, baby carrots, shiitake mushrooms, taro, and sweet potato—out of the fridge. Most of the veggies come directly from her home garden. She chops and dices the vegetables, tossing them with olive oil, garlic powder, and salt, and places them on a large cookie sheet lying on the kitchen's center island before popping them in the preheated oven to roast.

Tonight's dinner will be a mixed green salad with red onion, candied walnuts, goat cheese, and a Meyer lemon vinaigrette, followed by grilled ono served with mango and pineapple relish and roasted veggies.

Kate places the large salad minus the dressing in a bowl in the fridge. Next, she lays out the roasted veggies on a large platter on the kitchen island, covering them with tin foil. The wall clock indicates Kai will be home in roughly half an hour. Her husband's superior grilling skills will ensure the freshly purchased ono will taste delicious.

With time to spare before dinner, Kate heads toward her home office and powers up her laptop. On the car ride home from Dr. Yoshida's office, thinking about her ancestry search to find out more about her father's Irish-English side of the family has kindled Kate's interest in learning more about her mother's Italian line.

Kate shoots an email to her brother, Derek. She also uses this opportunity to share some recent beautiful photos of her trip to the Kohala Coast, ask about her nieces— Dawn and her younger sister, Ashley—and inquire when Derek and his wife, Julie, will visit.

Next, Kate invites her dad to dinner since his plans with his girlfriend, Jessie, were canceled when Malie called Jessie into The Plumeria Café to cover for a server taken ill.

Kate first met Jessie after Olivia and Malie invited Jessie to join Nā Pīkake. At the time, Jessie had been a new hire at The Plumeria Café. A former accountant in business with her late husband, Jessie had moved to Hawaii from the mainland after her husband tragically died in a car accident. Jessie and Glen, both having lost their beloved spouses after many happy years of marriage, found friendship in each other and, now, a blossoming love.

"This ono is delicious, Kai." Glen scoops up a piece of the succulent, honey-glazed white fish and Kate's fruit relish in the same bite.

"All the dinner dishes are quite a hit, my love." Kai leans over to Kate, pursing his lips, and Kate plants a big one on his lips.

"By the way, Dad," Kate says, "I'll be using my DNA to trace the relatives on Mom's side. The maternal lineage can be traced through either a male or female child. I've also started researching Taormina, where Mom's relatives lived. What a fascinating history and such a beautiful area. "

"Yes, it is. Stunningly beautiful and a place of inspiration for artists and writers," informs Glen.

"Growing up, I remember Mom telling me how her great-grandfather Leonardo Ricci came over through Ellis Island from Italy."

"That's right," says Glen. "Leonardo was in his early twenties when he came to America. He lived a long, happy life. I got to meet him. Although quite old at the time, he attended your mother's and my wedding just before he passed. He was a charming man."

"Did other family come over from Italy to America?" asks Kai as he takes another sip of his iced tea.

"Not that I know of," answers Glen. "Kate's mother's relatives in Italy ran a prominent import/export business. They exported all types of goods—oils, cheeses, wines—from Sicily to various ports worldwide. Leonardo admitted to me that he had an adventurous spirit and heard so many amazing things about America that he wanted to try to make a go of it here. So he opened up grocery stores in Boston."

"When I was little, I remember getting lots of yummy treats— like cannoli— when we visited my mother's parents, Gram Mary and Grampa Leo," reminisces Kate.

"That would be memorable." Kai chuckles, remembering the taste of the lemon-flavored ricotta cheese and chocolate morsel-filled tubes of deep-fried buttery pastry dough. "I loved the ones we ate when we visited Boston's North End."

"Cannoli certainly are a well-loved *Sicilian* treat," agrees Glen.

Several weeks later on a Saturday afternoon, after Kate's DNA results have been input into the Generation site, Kate peruses her mother's ancestral family tree. While recognizing most names, she discovers something entirely unexpected about her great-great grandfather Leonardo Ricci's lineage. *Grandpa Leonardo had a half-brother? Could my mother's relatives have kept a family secret?*

Kate thinks back to a year ago when she and Olivia attended the London Book Fair and how Kai joined her in Europe afterward. Having heard rumors that her father's relatives were Irish lords and ladies in centuries past, Kate and Kai traveled to Ireland for a vacation and did some ancestral research on her family's paternal side. Kate's investigations led her to discover and reaffirm this truth—that they were indeed related to Irish and English royalty—and also something entirely unexpected: the unearthing of a century-old family mystery. Kate's diligence led to a successful closure of the long-held familial secret and introduced the family to long-lost relatives.

Now, determined to find out more about her Italian lineage, Kate delves deeper.

6

Taormina, Province of Messina, Italy, 1868

"Beautiful, Lorenzo." Annabella examines her student's work as they sit in front of their painter's easels on the Ricci's terrace patio with its panoramic view of Taormina and the surrounding azure ocean.

Lorenzo's mother, Regina, sits in the background in her wheelchair, reading. She often looks up from her book to watch the art lesson.

Lorenzo's passion for drawing and painting has already produced beautiful creations for someone of his age, proving to Annabella that the boy has a natural talent. In addition she marvels at the seriousness with which he approaches his studies.

Lorenzo's father and mother gifted their son with a gorgeous mahogany paint box to start his classes with Annabella. The box, fitted with brass hardware and exquisite leather lining, houses porcelain mixing pans, washbowls, brushes, and tins filled with charcoal, crayons, and blocks of ink.

Annabella starts each lesson with a bit of art history, then education on understanding the fundamentals: color, value, composition. For example, the medium Lorenzo is studying—watercolor—begins with understanding how the paint's pigments get diluted in water, making them liquid to spread across the paper. Annabella demonstrates how the colored pigments affix to the paper's surface as the paint dries and the water evaporates. She explains to Lorenzo that the ratio of pigment to water impacts the transparency: the more diluted the coloring, the lighter the tone of the brush marks. For darker tones, it is necessary to use less water, thus producing a higher dye concentration. Finally, Annabella explains three basic techniques, including using a wet brush on dry paper.

"This gives the painting sharp, clean edges and precise lines. Another technique is to paint on damp—but not soaking—paper." Annabella demonstrates how this method provides tremendous ease in blending colors and softer tones.

"And this technique—" Annabella dips her brush into the paint and applies it to the paper several times to add depth of color using a layering technique.

"I want to try." Lorenzo, excited, starts to paint. "Like this?" He layers a blue color on the page to create an image of water.

"Very good."

"I think that's enough of your lesson today," announces Regina about half an hour later.

"Mamma!" protests Lorenzo. He could paint for hours.

"You heard what I said, Lorenzo. It's time for your reading and other studies."

"It's okay, Lorenzo. I'll see you next Saturday," says Annabella as she and Lorenzo pack up the art supplies. "For your homework, continue working on your Taormina Coast painting."

Lorenzo, somber, nods.

"Lorenzo, now!" commands Regina sharply as Lorenzo's father, Giovanni, walks onto the terrace.

Lorenzo sighs and nods. He knows it's useless to argue with his mother. He hugs Annabella, then kisses his mother and father before heading inside the villa, following his mother's orders.

"Come, Annabella, let me walk you to your villa." Giovanni smiles, holding out his hand.

"Our butler, Nunzio, can do that." Regina's delivery is curt and sour.

"My dearest," Giovanni says lovingly to his wife. "I let Nunzio have a few hours off this afternoon to run an errand for his mother. We can't have Annabella walking the streets alone, can we? I, for one, doubt her parents would approve."

"Tsk." Regina clucks with disapproval but doesn't have a comeback, as she knows what Giovanni says is true. "Can't you take the carriage?"

"It's a beautiful day and a short walk."

Regina grumbles, but she knows she's not going to win this round.

7

Annabella and Giovanni's mile or so walk to her home is filled with laughter and light conversation.

He's so handsome, thinks Annabella as Giovanni's blue eyes sparkle. *And funny*. Giovanni's witty observations and comments about daily life in Taormina have Annabella laughing out loud.

"And when Signora Rossi found out her husband ate the box of *cassata* cakes," shares Giovanni as they pass the Rossi family bakery, "Oh, what a scene!" Giovanni shakes his hands and makes a funny face, eliciting another ripple of laughter from Annabella. "The entire town heard Signor Rossi scream for his life as his wife chased him down the street, shaking a wooden spoon."

"Oh, my!" Annabella holds her stomach. "You're making me laugh too much."

"What? No! One can never laugh too much. Besides, I enjoy watching you smile. You have a beautiful smile."

Annabella blushes.

"You do," insists Giovanni. "Come. Let's get some *cassata* cakes."

"No!" Annabella protests, but her grin says otherwise.

Giovanni takes Annabella's hand, crossing the street and into the Rossi bakery. "*Buongiorno*, Signora Rossi," Giovanni greets the plump woman behind the bakery counter with a toothy smile.

Signora Rossi, although an older woman, is not oblivious to Giovanni's charms. She straightens up and smooths her apron. "*Buongiorno*, Giovanni. So good to see you."

"Signora Rossi, I'd like to introduce you to my son's art teacher and my business partner's daughter, Annabella Costa."

"Yes, I know the Costas. Good morning to you, too, Annabella."

Annabella nods and smiles hello.

"I was telling Annabella how delicious your cassata cakes are," Giovanni explains.

Signora Rossi gushes. "*Grazie*, Giovanni."

"Yes, my wife's cassata cakes are a real treat!" Signor Rossi interjects, having just entered the store from a backroom.

Signor Rossi, half his wife's size, is a cute man with a head full of gray curly hair. Annabella, remembering Giovanni's description of how Signora Rossi chased her husband around the bakery for devouring a box of cassata cakes, bites her lip to suppress a smile. She can imagine how Signor Rossi might be afraid of his wife.

"And the cakes are *exclusively* for our shoppers," snaps Signora Rossi, as if remembering the incident.

"Yes, dear!" Signor Rossi salutes his wife, who scoffs at her husband's silliness.

Giovanni turns to Annabella and winks while Annabella has to fake a cough to hold back laughter. Then she turns her head and breathes deeply to regain her composure as Giovanni examines the delectable-looking round sponge cakes. The cakes, moistened with fruit juices and liqueur, layered with ricotta cheese, candied fruit, and covered in various colors of marzipan icing, are culinary wonders. Giovanni points to the confections he'd like boxed. Once assembled, he pays Signora Rossi, and he and Annabella proceed toward her home.

"My parents will love the cakes. Grazie." Annabella smiles broadly as she and Giovanni stroll the twists and turns of Taormina's stone streets.

"But of course." Giovanni's charm and smile intoxicate. His friendly, familiar demeanor makes Annabella feel like they've known one another forever. She is awed and surprised by the feelings he conjures in her. At each meeting with Giovanni, Annabella's body seems to fill with kinetic energy that causes her skin to tingle, her face to become flush, and her mind to race.

Annabella spends hours contemplating every word of their conversations. And then there are the lifelike dreams—hearing Giovanni's voice, reveling in his presence, gazing into his breathtaking blue eyes—only waking to discover the acute pain upon the realization that her feelings can never go anywhere. Giovanni is married with a child. Annabella admonishes herself for her girlish foolishness and commands such thoughts right out of her head.

8

———

"You're beautiful, *mio caro*, inside and out," whispers Stefano tenderly, pushing a strand of Annabella's flyaway hair from her face before taking hold of her hand. The couple is sitting on the Costas' terrace one night after dinner weeks later.

"I love you so much." Stefano's heart races as a gust of warm ocean breeze caresses the couple.

"I know." Annabella smiles and places her free hand on Stefano's, entwining their fingers. "I love you too, Stefano."

Getting down on one knee, Stefano pulls a ring from his pocket. It's a beautiful, oval diamond surrounded by blue sapphires on a 14K gold band. "Will you marry me?" he asks softly.

"Stefano!" gushes Annabella, surprised, although she has always known this day would come.

"I have your parents' blessing."

"Ah," sighs Annabella. "I thought we would have more time before we got engaged."

"You do want to marry me?" Stefano asks.

"It's not that … I just … I don't know if I'm ready to leave home quite yet."

Stefano chuckles. He knows how close Annabella is to her family—as much as he is to his.

Annabella, overcome, wipes a tear from her cheek.

"Oh, please don't cry." Stefano is more concerned for Annabella than himself.

"I just need some time … all right?" sniffs Anabella.

Stefano reaches out and embraces her. "Of course, my love. I'm not going anywhere," he assures her.

Annabella has always felt her destiny was Stefano. Stefano is a good man—kind, gentle, intelligent, extremely attractive, loving, and from an outstanding family. He's the perfect match, and they've known each other since they were children. Stefano makes Annabella feel safe, secure, and protected. So why, then, is Giovanni infiltrating Annabella's thoughts during the day and entering her dreams at night?

46

9

The art lessons with Lorenzo continue weekly, often culminating with conversations with Lorenzo and Giovanni over lunch or tea while Regina sleeps or keeps to her chambers. Dinners and evening walks with Stefano turn to talk of marriage and the Bianchi and Costa families. Annabella can't help but feel she is living in two worlds. She tries to push thoughts of Giovanni out of her mind, but they creep in anyway. Sometimes, she compares Stefano to Giovanni, and when she does, she admonishes herself.

"Art lessons again!" scoffs Regina as she maneuvers her wheelchair onto the terrace where Lorenzo paints with Annabella.

"Good afternoon, Signora Ricci." Annabella's warm greeting only elicits only a grunt from Regina.

"How are you feeling today, Mama?" asks Lorenzo, getting up from his easel to give his mother a peck on the cheek.

"Fine, my dear." Regina's warmth appears to extend only to her son.

Lorenzo takes up his paintbrush again but turns to ask, "When will Papa be home?"

"For dinner," replies Regina, opening a book.

Annabella's heart drops. That means she won't see Giovanni today. Her lesson with Lorenzo is almost over. Darkness descends on her heart, but moments later, it lifts with joy as Giovanni enters the terrace.

"Papa!" Lorenzo gets up and races into his father's arms.

"I thought you wouldn't be home until dinner?" says Regina, surprised to see her husband.

"The meeting got canceled." Giovanni dutifully kisses his wife's cheek.

"Well, I'm sure you're happy to see Annabella is still here." Regina scowls and says sharply, "Annabella, the lesson is over—"

47

"Mama, Anabella was going to show me how to—"

"Lorenzo, your father is home. It's family time. Anabella needs to leave," states Regina rudely. Regina's rude behavior leaves Giovanni stunned.

Annabella begins to pack her things.

"Come, I'll walk you out," Giovanni reaches for Anabella's bag of supplies.

"Nunzio can walk Annabella home, Giovanni," Regina shouts at Giovanni, but he and Annabella have already left the terrace.

"I am so sorry for my wife's attitude." Giovanni's eyes look pained. "She's not been feeling well. I want to walk you home, but I better let Nunzio."

"I understand. Grazie."

Later that night, getting ready for bed, Annabella's heart feels like a pin cushion pierced with needles. She aches—emotionally and physically. It's a mystery to her as to why her feelings for Giovanni are growing. Dare she believe his are for her as well? Perhaps that is why Regina treats her so. Does Regina sense something that Annabella and Giovanni dare not acknowledge?

"Signorina?" Later that night, Annabella's maid, Flora, knocks at the bedchamber door.

"Come in."

Flora sets the most stunning vase of bright pink and white long-stem roses on a table.

"Oh my!" exclaims Anabella, reaching for the envelope accompanying the arrangement. She reads the note:

Please accept these roses as a thank you for all you do and for your lovely spirit. We appreciate you. Lorenzo, Giovanni, and Regina Ricci

"How thoughtful." Annabella smiles as she looks up from the letter. "They're from the Riccis."

"They're lovely. May I fetch you anything before bed, my dear?"

"No, thank you, Flora. I will see you in the morning."

Several times during the night, Annabella awakens from romantic dreams involving Giovanni and frightening nightmares involving Signora Ricci and Stefano. After one such rude awakening, she opens her night table drawer and reaches for her Bible to find comfort and peace in his word. She finds it in Mark 10: 6-9.

"But from the beginning of the creation God made them male and female. For this cause shall a man leave his father and mother, and cleave to his wife; And they twain shall be one flesh: so then they are no more twain, but one flesh. What therefore God hath joined together, let not man put asunder."

The following day, Annabella is clear on what she must do to quiet her spirit—put to bed any romantic fantasies about Giovanni and crush her terrifying dreams.

"We delight in the beauty of the butterfly,
but rarely admit the changes it has gone
through to achieve that beauty."

~~Maya Angelou

10

Olivia and Kate peck away on their laptop keyboards in the spacious, peaceful, and beautiful comfort of Olivia's home office. They sit facing one another at two, large, dark Koa-wood desks surrounded by attractive, dark-wood shelving loaded with books, photos, and beachy crafts. Directly across from the open lanai slider, which looks out onto the backyard green and the still, azure ocean beyond, a large comfortable sofa-and-loveseat arrangement is visible.

A small kitchen with a long wooden table surrounded by wicker chairs used for working lunches and informal conferences is adjacent to their desks. Most days, Kate works out of the comfort of her home office. However, now also working with Olivia to develop and write stories for *Olivia!* magazine and, sometimes, brainstorm other business ideas, the ladies make it a point to get together for face-to-face workdays at least twice a week. They love the synergy, camaraderie, and laughs.

"I'm going to make another pot of coffee." Kate gets up from her desk and walks over to the office kitchen. "Care for a cup?"

"Must be the three o'clock hour," Olivia says with a chuckle. "Sure. FYI, I have those yummy all-natural chocolate-and-fruit nut bars in the fridge to the left."

"Oh, I'll go for one of those. I'm always game for treats minus processed sugar and preservatives. Ow!" Kate exclaims when she smacks her chest on the fridge door. "I've been such a klutz lately. Probably because I'm tired."

"You're not sleeping well?"

"Just okay. Maybe I'm just PMSing. I'm so tender all over, too."

"You'll feel better after coffee and chocolate."

Back at her desk Kate loses herself in her work as she sips her brew and eats her afternoon snack. However, about a half-hour later, her face is green. "I feel weird. Like I'm going to—" She runs to the bathroom, slamming the door.

Alarmed, Olivia gets up from her desk. "Kate?" Olivia knocks on the bathroom door. "Hey, girl, you okay?"

"NOT!" Kate opens the door with a pouty face. "I threw up."

"OMG, I wonder if you're coming down with something."

"I feel okay now."

Olivia feels Kate's forehead. "You don't have a fever, that's for sure. Do you want to lie down for a while?"

"No, I'm okay, really."

"When's your period due?"

Kate heads to her desk and looks at her datebook, counting the days and weeks. "Wow! I'm two weeks late."

"Seriously?"

Kate nods.

"Well, girlfriend, if you want to, go to the drugstore asap and pick up a pregnancy test—" Olivia looks at her watch. "We've got a few hours before our Nā Pīkake sisters arrive."

Following a quick trip to the drugstore and back to Olivia's, Kate follows the instructions on the pregnancy test packaging.

"We've got another minute." Olivia holds the plastic pregnancy-detection device, watching for two pink lines in the window indicators as Kate paces.

"Don't tell me anything. Just let me see the strip when it's time."

"Okay, it's time." Following Kate's direction, Olivia does not indicate the results as she hands the device to Kate.

"OMG!" screams Kate. "I'm pregnant!"

Both ladies proceed to bounce around the room as they scream for joy.

"I'm going to be an auntie! Woo-hoo!" enthuses Olivia.

"I should call Kai." Kate, still shaking, comes to a standstill. "No, I'll drive to the ER to see if he has a moment. I can't wait for him to get home tonight—he said he'd be late. I'll be a basket case. Oh. Oh. He's going to be so excited!"

"Come on. I'll drive. You just breathe deep and relax," commands Olivia as both ladies grab their purses and head for Olivia's car.

"Oh, babe, this is so fantastic!" Kai, alone with Kate in a quiet room at the hospital, pulls Kate close and hugs her before they share a kiss.

"It feels like a dream. I'm so happy," gushes Kate.

"Me, too." Kai pulls Kate even more tightly against himself and kisses her again. "We should set up an appointment asap with your OB-GYN."

"Already on it. I called and made an appointment for later this week."

"Excellent. Do you want to wait to tell folks until the first trimester is over?"

"No!" cries Kate, excited. "I can barely contain myself now. I won't tell the world, just our fathers, Malie, and . . . I know I'll have to share the news tonight with my Nā Pīkake sisters, but that's it. A small circle. Let's call our fathers together now if you have time."

"Great idea," Kai strokes Kate's hair and beaming face. "I love you so much."

"And I love you." Emotional again, Kate wipes a tear from her eye before it can travel down her cheek. "Must be the hormones."

Kai pulls Kate close again. They silently stand and hold one another, reveling in the good news for a moment before sharing it with their ohana.

Daahling, this is simply fantastic news!" exclaims Elaine Harrison as she hugs Kate later that evening in Olivia's great room before the Nā Pīkake meeting commences. "We're all going to be aunties! I love it!"

"Ah, let me get one thing clear, ladies," Olivia announces to everyone gathered—Elaine, Kate, Malie, Alana, Jessie, and Sukey—"I've already proclaimed myself as Auntie Number One!"

"I'm number two," screams Malie, laughing.

"Three," chuckles Sukey.

Alana and Jessie become four and five, respectively. The room breaks out in more laughter as the women celebrate Kate's good news.

"This is going to be one well-loved baby," says Kate, who starts to tear up again, her emotions taking center stage. "You all mean so much to me."

"Have a drink, daahling!" exclaims Elaine, holding up her champagne flute. "Oh, wait, no alcohol until the baby arrives. Another club soda and lemon?"

"Sure." Kate is smiling now and happily settled on the couch between her sister-in-law Malie and BFF Olivia.

"Another chocolate truffle, perhaps?" asks Olivia.

"Are you trying to fatten me up before my time?" Kate raises her eyebrows in question. "Well, one more couldn't hurt." She dives into the beautiful box of chocolate delights sitting on the coffee table and chooses one with a chewy coconut center clustered with almonds.

"Looks like we'll be planning a baby shower before our next fundraising event," Sukey remarks as she dips her fork into a beet-and-goat-cheese salad that she has piled high on her plate. The buffet table for the lady's dinner meeting boasts an array of healthy salads, grilled fish, and a variety of roasted veggies.

"Oh, yes, let's discuss," agrees Olivia before sipping her Arnold Palmer. "A shower date, and now, considering Kate's news, the theme of fostering family relationships for the next the Nā Pīkake fundraiser is on target!"

11

Taormina, Province of Messina, Italy, 1868

Lorenzo pouts as he dips his paintbrush into pot of custom-mixed indigo blue. He strokes his painter's canvas with the dark pigment to represent the calm Ionian Sea surrounding his family's terrace then pauses to brush a tear from his cheek with his forearm.

"Please understand, Lorenzo." Annabella's voice is soothing as she strokes Lorenzo's back. I've been accepted into a one-of-a-kind class to study art with the great Fritz Gromann."

"Who is he anyway?"

"A wonderful painter from Germany now living in Taormina."

"Why is he so great?"

"He paints stunning landscapes of our beautiful town."

"So?"

"He paints with oils on canvas. I know there is much I can learn from him."

"It will be like how you've been teaching me?"

Annabella rubs Lorenzo's back again as she nods.

"I see." Lorenzo's lips begin to quiver again as he attempts to hold back tears. "Will I be able to see you sometimes?"

"Of course. I'll still be living in Taormina."

Lorenzo cracks a small smile now that he knows he can always reach out to Annabella.

Giovanni walks Annabella back to her villa in quiet contemplation and finally breaks the silence. "Lorenzo was heartbroken when he learned his studies with you will be suspended."

"I know. I told him it was only for a season and that I wasn't leaving Taormina."

"I know he will miss your weekly visits." Giovanni sighs and kicks a pebble in his path.

Annabella notices Giovanni's face looks pained. *His face looks like my heart feels.* And she can't help but think, *Please, God, help me. Keep me strong.*

No more words are spoken as Annabella and Giovanni continue their walk, but Annabella's mind is reeling.

Unbeknownst to Annabella, Giovanni's mind is reeling as well. "Please, do not be a stranger." Giovanni manages a meager smile as they arrive at the front gate of Villa Maria. He takes Annabella's hand and kisses it. "Grazie, for everything."

Annabella nods in acceptance and manages a goodbye smile before disappearing behind the gated villa entrance.

12

Hanalei, Kauai, Present Day

In her dream Kate senses the presence of someone following her. She feels a change of energy in the atmosphere, then notices a black swish from the corner of her eye, but no one is there. When she wakes moments later, her eyes land on the digital clock sitting in front of her on the nightstand.

The illuminated numbers on the clock's face read 3:00 a.m. Kate sighs, now awake. She scoots closer to her sleeping husband and, feeling the delicious warmth from his body, soon falls back into a deep and comfortable sleep.

Upon waking a few hours later at her usual 6:30, Kate heads toward the Weke cottage's cheery kitchen and opens the shutters. It's a typical Hanalei morning—the ground is damp, and the sky is slightly overcast after an early morning shower. However, the rays of sun peeking through the mist will surely burn off the haze within the next few hours. Kate spoons a few heaping tablespoons of The Plumeria Café Kauai-coffee blend into a grinder, then places the fragrant grounds into a filter-lined basket in the kitchen's coffeemaker. She sighs with anticipation as the water begins to brew, walks over to the kitchen slider, and opens the door to greet the morning air.

"Aloha!" Kate calls out to the singing 'Apapane and I'iwi birds as she steps out onto the lanai. Walking down the garden path, she breathes deeply, relishing the scents and colorful blossoms from the plumeria trees planted to honor her mother, Catherine, and Kai's mother, Leilani, and the red, white, and yellow hibiscus and cascading, multi-colored rainbow treats. There are also greens and palms in several varieties. Sizeable Swiss cheese monstera deliciosa and blood-orange, green, and yellow ti plants are just a few beauties that grace the garden.

"I'll be back!" Kate calls out again to her leafy friends before heading back into the kitchen, anticipating the rich dark warmth of her wake-up cup of coffee.

Early morning times like this, while most of this part of the world still sleeps, and most definitely, Kai, at least for another hour, Kate enjoys her morning rituals. Coffee, safe doctor-approved exercise now that she's pregnant, more coffee, a walk in the garden sipping her brew as she contemplates her day and to-do list, and engaging in talks with God about whatever dreams made themselves known upon waking.

Who could I have been sensing following me in my dream? Although Kate had seen no one, she had felt a benign male presence. "Okay, God, if I'm meant to know more, please reveal it to me."

Her thoughts then turn to the little one growing inside her womb. "Hey, little one in my tummy, this is your mama speaking." Kate chuckles, thinking she might get committed if anyone saw her talking to her stomach. "Your daddy and I are looking forward to meeting you."

Kate shares her feelings, thoughts, and dreams with her unborn three-month-old for the next few minutes before returning to the kitchen to refresh her coffee.

Inside, she finds that Kai is up, and over a breakfast of homemade pancakes topped with organic coconut-vanilla yogurt mixed with fresh pineapple, strawberries, and mangos that they whip up from one of Kate's recipes on her gardenofaloha.com site, the lovers chat about the best way to spend their cherished "free" Saturday.

Kate's father, Glen, soon appears from the ohana guest cottage. "Aloha, young lovers!" he calls with a wave.

"Morning, Poppy. Care to join us in some pancakes? We made plenty."

"Yum. Don't mind if I do."

"You sit, sweetheart. I'll fix your father a plate," commands Kai, relaxed and happy to have a day free of his ER responsibilities.

"I'll follow you inside to grab a cup of coffee," says Glen.

Kate chuckles. "I could get used to this being pregnant." She loves how attentive Kai and her father have been to the expectant mother.

When the two men return, Kate turns to her father as they all enjoy their breakfast. "How's life at The Plumeria Café's market?"

"Couldn't be better. I even get to brag about the farm-to-table produce I take in after tending to it in this garden." Glen spreads his arms wide. The Weke garden is most impressive in its assortment of tomatoes, onions, leafy greens, taro, and other items that entice residents and travelers into the Café market.

"Well, Poppy, I'm sure you talk up the customers, and I know they appreciate the tasty produce, tenderly harvested with aloha." Suddenly, Kate grips her abdomen in distress.

"What is it, babe?"

"I'm not sure." After a second, the pain passes, only to revisit several minutes later. When Kate stands, Kai notices her white cotton PJs are stained with blood.

"Oh, no," cries Kate, shocked.

Kai doesn't waste a minute. "We're going to the ER *now*."

In a private hospital room, Kai holds Kate as she sobs in his arms. Kate's OB-GYN, Dr. Yoshida, unable to do anything more for Kate, lets the couple know to reach out to her if they need anything.

"Mahalo, Dr. Yoshida," says Kai and turns his attention back to Kate.

"Please stay with me," Kate pleads, then sobs even harder.

"Honey, I'm not going anywhere."

"I'm so sorry." Kate continues to cry. "I lost our baby. Our son."

"Sweetheart, there's no need to be sorry. Sometimes, a miscarriage is the body's way of saying something was off."

"I want to have a child."

"We'll try again. We'll have faith. God will guide us."

Kate's eyes begin to look heavy. The meds are doing their job. "If I fall asleep, stay with me."

"I'll be stuck like glue." Kai kisses Kate's forehead and caresses her back. "I love you so much, honey."

Kate, still teary, grasps Kai tightly.

13

Hanalei, Kauai, Present Day – Several Weeks Later

In her dream, Kate walks down Weke Road. The morning is bright, and the warmth of the sun's rays on her bare shoulders is a delicious sensation. The cacophony of chirps and hoots from the singing birds makes her smile. Then, a stunning and large Fritillary butterfly with glorious, deep-orange wings sporting silver and black spots makes a dive in front of her, prompting Kate to jump.

Kate chuckles. "Well, aloha to you too!" She follows the road toward the Hanalei Pier, where she will make her customary run before breakfast. A moment later, she hears gravel crunching underfoot behind her and turns. No one is there. Still, although she is the only person on the road, she senses the presence of another. Her dream then mutates into another scene where she sees a young man—twenty-something—who waves at Kate.

Kate sits up in her bed, wide awake. *Who was that?* She did not recognize the face of the young man, but he appeared friendly enough. *Curious.*

Her digital nightstand clock reads 5:55 a.m., five minutes before her natural body-clock always wakes her. Kai is working a double shift, so she's alone in their large king-size bed. With a giant yawn, Kate spreads across the sheets, flipping, flopping, and stretching her body awake while planning her day: coffee, a walk down Weke Road to the pier for a beach run, breakfast, more coffee, perusing the floral beauties and discovering new growths in their garden, then writing in her home office.

Kate enjoys the structure of her days, which occasionally alter when she works from Olivia's or tends to something unexpected. Routine has been a boost in helping her to heal from her recent miscarriage, although she has a ways to go. Of late, little, unrelated things make her cry at the drop of a hat. Sometimes, she's uncharacteristically short-tempered. She doesn't want to socialize, preferring a good book, a quiet evening, or an early slumber. Kai has been so loving and caring. If something wonderful can come out of such a disappointment, it's her realizing the depth of Kai's love and commitment. Kate's family and friends have been fantastic, too, letting her know they're sorry, showing they care in kind deeds and listening without saying a word—allowing Kate to express herself only when she feels like it.

Kate's thoughts are interrupted when she hears her cell phone's tropical music ring. "Aloha."

"Hey, babe, I've got a surprise for you," says Kai playfully on the other end of the call.

"You do?" Kate is immediately pleased and intrigued.

"How do you feel about some R and R?

"Okay …"

"Like a weekend getaway to Maui?"

"Seriously?"

"I know how much you love The Orchid."

"OMG!" screams Kate with delight.

The five-star hotel along the Wailea Beach Path, a narrow, oceanfront walkway that strings together a few high-end hotels with glorious, panoramic water views and easy beach access, is one of Kate's favorite vacation spots on Maui.

"Only the best for you, *e ku'u aloha*."

The words "my love" put a broad smile on Kate's face. She loves it when Kai speaks to her in Hawaiian, and the idea of spending a relaxing weekend together makes her spirits soar. It's just what they need.

"Get packin', hon! Our flight's early in the morning," Kai says before hanging up.

Excited, Kate pulls their luggage from the hall closet and starts to pack a mix of casual and dressy items while making a list of a few essentials to pick up at the market. Around lunchtime Olivia calls and asks Kate to meet her for an impromptu meal at The Plumeria Café. Kate is game. She feels her spirits rise.

As is usual, when Kate arrives at the café, it is packed with locals and visitors alike. The café, located in the center of Hanalei, features a lush garden with breathtaking views of the high peak mountain wonders of

Hihimanu, Namolokama, and Mamalahoa. The large, open, wooden plantation shutters and strategically placed ceiling fans allow a glorious breeze to filter through the upscale island-style eatery. Decorated in rich Koa woods and tropical patterns, it's a warm, inviting place to enjoy a relaxing breakfast or lunch or indulge in a delectable pastry while sipping a frothy cappuccino.

"Aloha, Malie!" Kate waves to her sister-in-law behind the café's tempting bakery counter. Busy tending to customers, Malie smiles and points Kate to the lanai where Olivia is waiting.

"What's that?" Kate points to a pretty gift bag decorated in a green-and-white tropical leaf pattern.

"It's for you, *ka'u hoaloha*." Olivia uses the Hawaiian words for "my friend" and hands Kate the package.

"You're speaking Hawaiian and smiling like a Cheshire cat. It must be something special."

Olivia chuckles. "Open it and you'll find out."

Kate pulls the rectangular package out of the gift bag and begins to remove layers of tissue paper. "Ah!" she gasps, stunned at the sight of a gorgeous 16 x 20 oil painting of Sicily's Taormina Coast. "Is this what I think it is?"

Olivia beams.

"It can't be." There's no doubt in Kate's mind that the painting is an original Fritz Gromann. Gromann, of German descent, fell in love with Italy's magical Taormina during a visit in the 1800s and ended up living in the area. He created beautiful oils of the breathtaking city and coast. "How did you—?" Kate stumbles to find her words.

"Ah, well, there's a tale."

"Spill."

"You know I recently interviewed a well-known art dealer for the Art Scene section of *Olivia!*"

"Yes ..."

"I mentioned that a friend, aka *you*, were doing some research on her maternal relatives via the Generation site and came across some gorgeous oils done in the late 1800s by Gromann. When I shared how taken you were with their beauty and the magnificent Taormina coast, one thing led to another, and the dealer practically gave me the painting.

"What? Oh, but the painting is too expensive. I can't accept it."

"Nonsense. I told you, the dealer practically gave it to me. All I had to do was give him some press. So I've made him an art expert for the publication. One hand washes the other."

"You are quite the wheeler and dealer. Mahalo. It's magnificent," Kate says, happily accepting the gift, and both of them laugh aloud at her obvious pleasure.

Kate leans over and hugs Olivia then carefully. Then she rewraps the gift in its packaging and securely places it on the empty chair next to her.

"How's the family research coming?" asks Olivia, sipping her iced tea.

"Still more to uncover. I'm really enjoying reading about Taormina's history. Did you know that in the nineteenth century, it became known as a city for literature and art? Not only did Gromann find inspiration from the geography and architecture of the gorgeous city, but it was also visited by Tennessee Williams, Truman Capote, Picasso, and so many others.

"You sound inspired just talking about it. Do you think you'll go and do some firsthand family research?"

"Well, gee, I didn't even think of that. But I like the idea."

"Maybe a vacation for you and Kai this year?"

"Mmm. I'll have to ponder that and ask Kai." Then, after a few moments, Kate makes a suggestion. "I'll tell you what would be really fun—me, Kai, you, and Grant hanging out in Italy as we did in England after last year's London Book Fair."

While Olivia filmed interviews with talent attending the book fair, Kate was on hand to cover print stories for *Olivia!* magazine. The timing for Kate couldn't have been better because she was in the middle of tracing her paternal relatives in England and Ireland.

The trip was highly successful for both women, both professionally and personally. The shows taped in England were rating winners, and Kate's engaging print articles also received acclaim. The number of likes and shares for Kate's pieces went into the high six digits in the magazine's online version. On the personal side, Kate and Kai meet new family members on a fun-and mystery-filled European vacation. Olivia and Grant also benefited from some quality, much-needed downtime.

"Let's keep that thought percolating," Olivia suggests as they order lunch.

As she eats her Caesar salad and a succulent piece of blackened grilled salmon, Kate instinctively senses eyes on her. She glances to her left, where other tables are situated on the lanai, and finds a young, twenty-something man staring at her. He's handsome and clean cut. As soon as he catches Kate's eye, he picks up his newspaper and starts to read it. *Where have I seen him before?* Kate wonders for a moment before shrugging it off.

"Love bears all things, believes all things, hopes all things, endures all things. Love never ends.

~~1 Corinthians 13:7

14

Maui, Hawaii, Present Day

The following morning, Kate and Kai board an early morning flight from Lihue to Maui's Kahului airport. They pick up their luggage and a white Ford Mustang convertible rental and then journey toward their resort destination.

"Ah." Kate sighs deeply as she and Kai begin their twenty-six-or-so-mile trip along the Pi'ilani Highway to their Wailea hotel. The thought of spending a romantic weekend away from her daily routine is entirely relaxing. "This trip is just what the doctor ordered."

Kai grinned. "I know, that's why I booked it."

"Cute." Kate chuckles at the phrase she frequently uses when referring to something of note Kai recommends. She breathes deeply and brushes back the hair the wind has strewn around her face. Feeling light and free, the change of pace and the gorgeous, lush, and expertly manicured landscape boosts her spirits and infuse a new sense of well-being within her. Although her recent miscarriage is still a heartbreak, she hopes she's stepping closer to healing ground.

Kai whistles as he drives, unaware Kate is staring. His whistling indicates that he's happy and content.

It warms Kate's heart that her honey is feeling so good. She chooses to remember every visual and emotional feeling of this moment in time, photographing it in her mind for later recall.

Thank you, God, for this wonderful man, this amazing day, and all that I have. She breathes deeply again. Her heart is full.

As they approach the hotel's sizeable paved pathway that leads under an imposing porch overhang with large white columns, Kate smiles when she sees the beautiful palms, plumeria, and ti plants surrounding the two cascading waterfalls on either side of the main entry. The hotel, although quite expansive, has a glamorous and intimate feel reminiscent of driving up to a private estate. Once the couple checks in, they head to their private beach bungalow.

Behind a pair of beautifully carved wooden doors surrounded by stucco walls, Kate and Kai survey their private oasis. A paved, irregular stone path bordered by colorful hibiscus hedges leads up to the front door. Immediately upon entering, Kate runs to a tropical arrangement that greets them in the foyer. She removes the envelope attached to the bouquet. "The arrangement is from my Nā Pīkake sisters and their husbands, wishing us a beautiful weekend."

"Boy, they don't skip a beat, do they?"

Kate smells the sweet plumeria, pikake, and other delicious aromas in the thoughtful gift.

"Look at the view!" Kai exclaims. The great room reveals a retractable wall framing an expansive beach-and-ocean vista beyond the foyer. The room is decorated in soothing hues featuring tropical flora. It features a wood-beam ceiling, a large L-shaped, overstuffed white linen sofa, a massive wooden coffee table, and a loveseat. Adjacent is a beautifully appointed kitchen. In the center, attractive high-back upholstered chairs surround a quartz center island. Comfortable wicker chairs surround the nearby rectangular dining table made of Koa wood.

"This place is amazing, Kai!" Kate opens the retractable great room wall to let in the ocean breezes. Additional seating and dining areas are arranged under a wooden pergola on the lanai.

After unpacking, the lovers head toward the resort's infinity pool with its ocean view and score two lounge chairs with a table under a large umbrella.

Once settled under the umbrella, a dip in the pool is the first order of business. Kai swims laps while Kate, holding on to a floating tube, leisurely doggie paddles. When she's had enough, Kate heads toward the set of lounge chairs they've chosen and lays out one of the resort's large, white, comfy beach towels. She plops down on the chaise and lets the sun dry her wet skin. The temperature is delightful.

"Aloha, Miss, may I get you something to drink?" asks a young waitress in a tropical-patterned sarong. She hands Kate a menu.

Once Kate has had a few moments to review the offerings, she orders two iced teas, a fruit bowl, and a pair of pineapple-coconut-mango scones. Even though she and Kai will be eating lunch in a few hours, Kate knows Kai will want something to nibble on to tide him over after his swimming workout. As for the scones, they are her guilty pleasure.

Waiting for the teas, Kate pulls a magazine she purchased from the resort's market out of her straw beach bag. The pages of the well-produced local magazine are filled with home decor spreads, healthy dinner recipe ideas, and lifestyle articles. Finally, Kate's gaze stops at an article—*The Healing Power of Nature*. She devours the piece for the next fifteen minutes, only picking her head up to sip her just-delivered iced tea.

According to the article, research shows being in nature can reduce stress-hormone levels, lower blood pressure, promote the immune-system response, improve mood, and reduce anxiety and depression. In addition, immersing oneself in nature encourages a positive sense of self and well-being, even facilitating creativity. The article further explains that our bodies and living cells are constantly working to regenerate. Therefore, being in nature for even small doses can facilitate immune and healing responses.

The article chronicles the stories of men and women who, after losing a loved one, experiencing the end of a marriage, facing job challenges and changes, and other scenarios, found extraordinary bodily and spiritual healing by being in nature. One woman, a city-dweller, even talked about how she rented a coastal-town cottage to heal after her child's death.

The stories she reads resonate with Kate. Being immersed in nature is something she has always found healing and rejuvenating. She has even written magazine articles about how research has shown that being in nature can help one's mental health, strengthen one's immune system, facilitate physical healing and concentration, lower blood pressure, and promote an overall feeling of well-being.

At the time of her first trip to Kauai, on assignment to interview Olivia for a *New York View* magazine profile piece, Kate's life did a 180 turn when her then-boyfriend Jason told her he'd never marry her after professing for five years that he would. That heartbreak was followed by the loss of Kate's dear mother, Catherine, to a brain tumor. The diagnosis came as a shock to the entire family, and Catherine passed away six weeks later. When Olivia learned of Kate's misfortunes and discovered how distraught Kate was, she offered Kate a cottage in Hanalei to rest and rejuvenate. That experience led to

Kate's introduction to Kai.

Kate remembers how carving out a few weeks of due vacation time to quiet her mind allowed her to regroup. Spending time in nature and appreciating her new ohana and the beauty of Hawaii led her to discover the healing mana of the Islands, not to mention learning to live in the spirit and "The Way of Aloha." She sighs at the memories.

How much my life has changed. Thank the Lord.

Kate shudders, thinking of past pain and losses, and she knows that while life presents many ups, downs, and challenges, it is essential not to lose hope and be open to love, forgiveness, and healing. It's simple but often hard to remember when upheaval and tragedy strike.

Kate's thoughts turn to her recent heartbreak—the child she lost. She and Kai had been so excited about being pregnant. Then planning the baby shower with her Nā Pīkake sisters and using decor inspirations from magazines to design a room for her newborn. Kate's stomach starts to churn. A visceral pain wells up inside her, and she can't hold back tears. Perhaps, wearing dark sunglasses and a large floppy hat, no one can see her cry. Tears flow down her cheeks, and she tries to wipe them away as fast as they fall. When Kate feels she's released all the hurt she's feeling inside, she digs into her beach bag, pulls out a tissue, and blows her nose.

Afterward, feeling the need to read God's word for solace, she opens the Bible app on her phone and navigates to Romans 15:13—*"Now the God of hope fill you with all joy and peace in believing, that ye may abound in hope, through the power of the Holy Ghost."* Kate re-reads the verse several times for comfort, then puts her phone down on the side table, closes her eyes, and falls asleep, exhausted from the emotional release.

Smooch. Kai kisses a sleeping Kate on the lips after emerging wet from the pool.

"Oh, your lips are cold and damp but delicious," she chuckles.

Kai, teasing, leans in for another peck. They kiss again, after which Kai plops onto his chaise. "What's this?" he asks, looking at the teas, fruit bowl, and partially eaten scones.

"A little something to tide us over until lunch."

"Thanks, pumpkin." Kai downs the tea and dives into the fruit bowl.

The next few hours are spent swimming, resting, and reading.

"I'm getting hungry again, honey bunny. Want to grab some

lunch?" asks Kai just after noon.

"I looked in the hotel's guide, and they have an excellent Asian Fusion place down the road a bit at the shopping plaza, but let's go shower and change first."

"I'm with you, babe."

Inside their bungalow, Kai closes the drapes in the master bedroom for privacy. He pulls his wet T-shirt over his head. Standing by the dresser, Kate removes her beach cover-up to reveal her bikini. Admiring his beautiful wife's physique, Kai feels a longing to touch her and walks over to the dresser where Kate stands.

Coming up behind Kate, Kai places his hands on Kate's shoulders and gently squeezes, massaging her neck and back.

"Mmm," moans Kate. "That feels good."

After several minutes, Kate's exposed neck is too delicious not to trace with kisses. The bare skin of their warm bodies touching is explosive. The moans continue.

"You feel so good." Kai turns Kate around for a deep soul kiss which melts her.

Lunch will have to wait.

15

Taormina, Province of Messina, Italy, 1868

In her dream Annabella walks a craggy stone path perched high above Taormina. The positioning gives her a spectacular view of the sea below—its waters aqua at the shoreline, morphing into deep gradient shades of blue as they lead to the ocean's depths. The sun's rays feel deliciously warm as they penetrate through her frock onto her skin. A gentle wind caresses her hair and shoulders. The sweet plumeria blossoms intoxicate. Except for an occasional opening or closing of a villa door, or distant conversation as residents break the fast on their balconies, only birdsong fills the air. Annabella loves her morning walks, which provide insights into life, her work, and her creativity. Then, from out of nowhere, she feels a masculine presence beside her. Curious, she turns to ascertain who it might be. *Giovanni!*

Giovanni smiles. His blue eyes pierce Annabella's soul. Taking Annabella's hand, Giovanni kisses it. The heat from his lips and touch creates a surge of electricity throughout her being. As they walk in silence, Giovanni continues to hold her hand.

Where am I? Annabella wakes, disoriented from her dream. She swallows hard as her eyes dart around the semi-darkened chambers.

Oh, it was a dream.

Shards of light peek through a slight opening in the heavy silk curtains framing the wooden terrace doors. No longer able to sleep, Annabella rises and puts on the satin robe draped over a nearby chair. She pulls the brocade sash to open the terrace door curtains as a knock sounds on her chamber door.

"Buongiorno, Bella," Annabella's maid, Flora, announces herself.

"Buongiorno, Flora. Come in." Annabella opens the terrace doors.

Flora is carrying a silver tray hosting a bowl of fresh fruit, warm crusty bread with a side of creamy butter, and an espresso—Annabella's favorite breakfast. She sets the tray on the terrace table that

74

faces a magnificent ocean view framed by stunning fuchsia bougainvillea.

As Annabella enjoys the solitude and beauty of the terrace, her thoughts return to her dream and the feelings Giovanni's presence and kiss evoked.

No! Annabella commands her mind to turn from such thoughts. Instead, she reminds herself that Stefano will be coming to dine tonight. Comforted by that realization, and looking forward to seeing Stefano, Annabella deliberately heads toward her wardrobe, where she ponders what outfit to wear. She finally settles on the pale peach chiffon which will be striking against her sun-kissed complexion.

After breakfast, Annabella follows her morning routine and returns to her artist's easel. Having started her classes with Fritz Gromann, she expertly strokes colors of pigment on the canvas to capture the beauty of the sun's golden light and the mesmerizing shadows they create. Her work also encompasses the lush, flowing vines that hang from the stone-and-wood pergola and the variety of planted and potted floral beauties surrounding the villa's terrace garden.

Later that afternoon, Annabella walks close to the villa to take respite from her painting. The fresh air and solitude are like sustenance for her soul.

"Annabella!" a man's voice rings out.

Hearing her name called, she turns around from her perch along the avenue's stone wall.

It's Giovanni!

Several weeks have passed since her final tutoring session with Lorenzo on the other side of town. Seeing Giovanni is a surprise.

"It's good to see you," speaks Giovanni. His eyes look sad and heavy.

Annabella nods, self-conscious.

"May I walk with you for a bit?"

Unsure how to respond, Annabella again nods.

"We miss you," Giovanni tells her.

"I … I miss you all as well."

They walk in uncomfortable silence for several minutes. Then, finally, each wants to talk, but neither knows how to express what's in their hearts.

"I didn't expect this to happen," begins Giovanni. Seeing Annabella flash him a questioning look, he continues, "I think you know what I'm referring to."

"Did you come looking for me today?" The look on his face tells her that she has guessed correctly.

"I had to see you one last time. I've never felt like this. My marriage with Regina was arranged by our families when we were children. She was a lovely person. I loved her as best I knew how at that young age. Then, a few years after Lorenzo was born, the accident happened. It caused her heart to harden—to everyone and everything."

"I'm so sorry."

"Then you came into our lives. You made me feel something I've never felt. And you made me laugh and feel very happy. At least once, I had to tell you that I love you." Giovanni starts to cry, and this causes Annabella to do the same. "I know that I am married, that I committed—"

"Yes, and you must honor that, as must I."

"I know," says Giovanni, still wiping tears from his cheeks. "I want to give you this. Lorenzo wanted you to have it and asked that I give it to you. To remember us."

Giovanni opens a velvet box, revealing a beautiful, white-gold flower bracelet—lilies encrusted with diamonds.

"Oh, I don't know—"

"Lorenzo picked it out especially for you."

Annabella starts to cry as Giovanni clasps the bracelet around her wrist.

"*Ti amo, amore mio.*"

"*Ti amo,*" Annabella sobs.

The couple holds each other tightly for several seconds. Then Giovanni kisses Annabella's forehead, cheeks, and lips. "I must go now. And it would be best if you find your life as well. I'm unsure of God's plan as my heart aches, but I know there is a reason."

"I believe that too."

"I am so grateful I met you."

"Me too." Annabella begins to tear up again.

"Try not to cry, *amore mio.*" Giovanni releases her hand and begins to back away. "Let me see you smile before I leave."

Annabella manages a smile as she waves goodbye.

16

Hanalei, Kauai, Present Day

In her dream Kate, happy, walks the shores of Anini Beach. A small object appears to rise out of the sand. *What is that?* She walks closer to get a better look. Suddenly, a child's form begins to emerge. It's a baby in silhouette. Scared, she gasps and wakes with a start, but brushes the dream of as a nightmare.

Several weeks since she and Kai enjoyed a relaxing escape to Maui, this morning is like any other. She can hear Kai showering as she throws on her silk robe and proceeds toward the kitchen to make Kai his breakfast—a to-go protein smoothie—which will give him enough energy to start his double shift in the ER.

After Kai leaves for the hospital, as usual Kate takes off on her morning run. Exiting the Weke cottage, she notices a young man sitting in a nondescript brown sedan across the street. Through his open window, the man sees Kate staring. He waves before he starts scrolling through his phone messages.

That looks like the young man I saw when I lunched with Olivia at The Plumeria Café. Could he be a tourist?

Jogging toward the Hanalei Pier, her thoughts turn to other subjects while she completes her hour-long run.

"Aloha!" the young man she saw earlier in the brown sedan waves to Kate as she walks up the stone path to the Weke cottage's front door. "I was wondering if Kai Stevens might be home?"

"Who's asking, please?"

"Oh, sorry, my name's Noah Blake."

"Does Kai know you?"

"Uh, no."

"What does this concern?

"One of his college friends—Dr. Hiroshi Kimura—mentioned Dr. Stevens might be willing to talk to me about what it takes to become an ER doctor. He gave me Dr. Stevens's contact information. I'm interested, you see—"

"Oh, yes, Hiroshi, he was Kai's college dorm mate. I'm curious, though. Why did you come here to talk to Kai rather than the hospital?"

"I figured, ah, well, him being an ER doctor. They're kind of busy at work, so——" Noah chuckles nervously.

That answer rings true. Even Kate knows it's best not to phone Kai at work but instead for wait for her husband to reach out when he's free. Kate always cringes at the thought of interrupting a potential life-or-death emergency. "Well, why don't you tell me how he can get in touch when he has time."

"Sure." Noah runs back to his car to grab a pen and paper. He jots down his information and hands Kate the piece of paper. "I appreciate it, ah, Mrs. Stevens?" The last is a question, as Noah seems to be unsure of Kate's identity.

"Yes, Kate Stevens."

"Thanks." Noah waves goodbye and returns to his car.

"He said his name is Noah Blake and that Hiroshi said you'd probably be open to talking to him about being an ER doctor," Kate tells Kai when he comes home that evening. She hands him the piece of paper inscribed with Noah's contact information.

"Oh, yeah! I remember now." Kai plops down on the great room couch, satisfied after enjoying a delicious dinner of grilled mahi-mahi tacos sweetened with a topping of pineapple and mango chunks. "Hiroshi sent me a text with Noah's contact info just before our trip to Maui. I forgot all about it."

"At first, he took me off guard. But he seemed rather sweet and gentlemanly. He kind of reminded me of you." Kate settles down next to Kai, wraps her arms around his waist and plants a kiss on his cheek.

"Well, if he reminded you of me, he must have been quite the awesome hunk," teases Kai.

Kate playfully bats Kai with a plush, decorative sofa pillow. The two love birds get into a frisky skirmish that turns to quite the tickle-fest. As is usual in these competitions, Kai is in the lead.

"No, stop. My dinner," Kate protests. "You don't want it ending up all over you, do you?"

"Ah, that would not be good. Okay then. Time out." Kai scoops Kate in his arms for a tender kiss.

"Much better," moans Kate.

17

"Here, I want you to have this." Kate's father, Glen, hands her a beautiful white-gold bracelet decorated in a pattern of diamond-encrusted flowers. "I buried it in my suitcase before I left New York. I almost forgot it was there."

"It's gorgeous. Mahalo, Poppy. I remember Mom wearing this."

"The bracelet was given to your mother by her grandmother, whose mother gave it to her."

"I love it." Kate studies the bracelet's intricacies. "The craftsmanship is superb."

Glen chuckles. "Like everything made of old."

"Are these lilies?" wonders Kate aloud as she continues to examine the work of art.

"I believe so."

"Wow. Remember the necklace with the white lilies I was gifted during my trip to Kona?" Kate pulls the chain from under her blouse to show her father.

"Yes. You said lilies had something to do with motherhood."
Kate sighs.

"I hope I didn't upset you, dear."

"No, Poppy. I'm okay. Maybe this bracelet is a sign of sorts. Whatever is meant to be, I know God has a plan. I hope being a mother is in store for me. But the important thing is to appreciate my blessings and what I have. And pray that if I'm meant to have children, it will happen when the timing is right."

"That's the spirit, my love. Come with me. Let's see how the lobster claw heliconia are coming along." The waxy flower bracts of the heliconia, bright red and tipped with splashes of vibrant yellow, hang in long racemes like pendants off abundant, glossy, dark green leaves. After almost a year of growth, the fast-growing exotic plants are thriving.

"They're beautiful, Dad."

As Kate and her father explore other garden beauties, Kate's

79

mind drifts to some of her first trips to the Islands. She had never laid eyes on such exotic flowers—the tropical birds of paradise, hibiscus in various hues from red, gold, pink, and orange, the torch-like jeweled ginger in red, yellow, and pink, the other-worldly Protea flower, the striking rainbow shower trees with their colorful cascading beauties, and of course, the sweet-smelling plumeria in shades of white and pink. She has made sure the Weke cottage garden features these gems and others, making it a unique family haven.

The family garden has been a place of solace following her mother's death, dealing with life's little anxieties and, even more recently, working through the grief of losing a child. So whenever she steps into the garden and stops to enjoy a cup of coffee or a sip of iced tea in the many seating areas of the Weke cottage's private oasis, she feels blessed. Thanking the Creator for the magnificence that surrounds her is a daily occurrence.

Later that afternoon, after a productive morning of writing magazine articles for *Olivia!* and several hours spent working on her next novel, Kate peruses the ancestry clues and files in her online Generations account. First, she views the paperwork of her third-great-grandfather Leonardo Ricci upon his arrival at Ellis Island. There's also a picture of him in one of the files. It's a clipping from an old newspaper that mentions him, his wife, Anna Maria, and their child, Gitano, Kate's great-great-grandfather, along with some other people disembarking from a ship at Ellis Island. Kate looks at the grainy image, remembering Leonardo's handsome face from a few old family photos. He was a stunner.

Kate remembers her mother talking about Italian emigration to the United States. If memory served, Italians began emigrating in significant numbers in the 1860s, with the greatest number in 1907. They came—most of them via Ellis Island–seeking a better quality of life and labor opportunities. However, Leonardo's reason for relocating to the States was due to the devastating earthquake that rocked Sicily on December 28, 1908. The quake—it would have registered as a 7.5 on today's Richter scale—caused tsunamis, fires, and landslides that devastated Messina and Reggio Calabria. Several members of the Ricci family and friends perished, which prompted Leonardo's wife, Anna

Maria, to insist they seek safer ground. The couple wound up making their home in Boston. Shortly after arriving in the States, Leonardo Ricci opened what would become a well-known grocery chain that imported goods from Italy.

For the next few hours, Kate works on collecting more clues to identifying relatives in her extensive family tree. She jots down the names of hints that pop up as still living on the east coast of Sicily in the hilltop town of Taormina and various other Italian locales.

18

"Another superb dinner fit for a king!" As he sits at the lanai table overlooking the Weke cottage garden, Kai raises his arms for a stretch.

"We make a pretty good team—you helping with the prep and grilling," says Kate, removing dishes from the table.

Kai starts picking up the remaining plates from the table. "I'll wash. You wipe."

Kate nods in agreement.

"Oh, I almost forgot, that young man, Noah Blake. I called him. He asked if he could drop by after dinner tonight. Okay with you?"

"Sure, what time were you thinking?"

"Oh, about eight. It will probably only be for an hour or so."

"Great. Want to wait and serve dessert then?"

"Sounds like a plan." Kai plants a kiss on Kate's lips.

About a half hour before Noah's arrival, Kate slices up a blend of mango, strawberries, kiwi, pineapple, and papaya. She places the fruit salad in a large decorative bowl, tossing the mix with freshly squeezed lemon juice before putting the dish in the fridge to chill.

"I'll get it." Kai answers the front door when the bell rings some twenty minutes later.

After their greetings, Kai and Kate show Noah onto the lanai. White solar lights, strategically hanging from the lanai roof, surrounding palms, and throughout the garden, sparkle, magically illuminating the yard.

"Your place is beautiful," admires Noah.

"Mahalo," Kai says as he and Noah sit at the lanai table set for dessert. "Where would you like to start? What can I share about working as an ER doctor?"

Noah waits to reply as Kate brings out a tray with the fruit salad and a carafe of coffee, placing them at the center of the table. Once she is seated, Noah, looking deeply perplexed, begins, "Well … um, I'm wondering just how to mention this, Dr. Stevens…"

"It's okay. We don't bite," Kai jokes to lighten the mood.

Noah chuckles nervously. "My mother recently passed away."

"I'm sorry to hear that," says Kai.

"As am I," adds Kate. "My mother passed away a few years back, so I know how that feels."

"Mine, too. So I do as well," says Kai.

"Thank you," acknowledges Noah. "My mom told me something before she passed, something she kept secret. I don't think there's any right way to say this. So, I'll just come out with it. Dr. Stevens, *I'm your son.*"

"What?" Kai's eyes bulge and Kate gasps.

"Growing up, I thought my parents split up because they didn't get along. My mom didn't say anything to dispel that belief. However, just before she died, she finally told me the truth—she had in-vitro with donor sperm."

The moment is all too surreal. Kate looks questioningly at Kai, wondering what this has to do with Kai. "Kai?"

"During medical school, I, um, donated once. I knew someone at the lab, but I told them afterward that I had changed my mind, for many different reasons. The specimen was destroyed but perhaps not as soon as I thought."

Kate, in shock, swallows hard. How … why do you think Kai is your biological father?"

"DNA testing and research on an online ancestry site."

"Generations?" Kate sighs when Noah nods. "Oh my, Kai. You did the test, but we haven't yet examined your family tree." Kate's nervous energy forces her to stand. "And here I've been researching my mother's family tree. I wonder what other surprises will turn up now that DNA testing and tracing are available to the masses." Kate starts to pace but Kai is eerily quiet.

"I'm sorry for disrupting you. I know this is a lot to take in. I'll go." Noah stands, as does Kai.

"Look, please try to understand. We have to get our bearings right now," says Kai.

Noah nods. He obviously gets it. "I understand."

"What about Hiroshi? You said you called him. Did you tell him about the DNA results?"

"No, I just told him what I told you, that I wanted to learn more about being an ER doctor."

"Do you really, or was that something you said to find me?"

"I *am* pre-med, but my main reason was to meet you."

Thinking about what to do and say, Kai runs his hands through his hair. "Noah, I, ah, my wife and I need a little time alone to process what you've told us. I hope you understand."

"Of course. I need to get going anyway."

"I'll be in touch with you in the next day or two, okay?" Kai squeezes Noah's shoulder as they walk toward the front door. He closes the door and, turning, looks sheepishly at Kate, who is fighting back tears.

"A sperm donor?"

"I wasn't thinking about the potential ramifications. When I finally did, I asked that my sample be destroyed. I thought it was—and it was—but I guess not all of it."

Kate's silence is deafening.

"It was all so different back then. There was anonymity."

"Yeah, well, that was then." Kate inhales and exhales quickly in succession. She's still pacing.

"I didn't intend for this to happen."

"I'm sure. But it has. And what does it mean? What do you think he wants? Is he now our responsibility? Are we supposed to make him part of our family now?" Kate starts to cry.

Kai wants to hug Kate, but she raises her hand, keeping him away.

"Look. The first thing we'll have to do is do another DNA test to confirm."

"That would be wise, and yes, I agree. But now that I know this, when you look at Noah, he's your spitting image. So at least someone was able to give you a son."

"Kate. Stop!" Kai doesn't want to hear this kind of crazy talk. "Don't think like that." Then, looking at his wife, who is obviously in pain, he speaks tenderly. "We'll have other chances."

"Will we? My biological clock has almost run out." Kate sits on the sofa, defeated.

"That's not true, but we are still obviously in mourning." Kai sit down next to his wife, and this time, Kate allows his embrace. They hold on to one another, sobbing.

"You'll get through this, my friend." Olivia hugs Kate several days later. The ladies sit on Olivia's lanai.

"If I were in Noah's place, I'd probably want to find out who my parent was," says Kate, still processing.

"Let's go for a walk by the water. Communing with nature does a soul good."

The ladies head down the stone stairway from Olivia's backyard to the serene waters at the ocean's shore.

The pair walk in silence, both listening to the melodic sounds of the tide's ebb and flow and the occasional chirping of birds in the trees.

"Mahalo for listening to me."

"You're going through a lot. I want to be here for you just like you were there when I reunited with my birth child, Alia."

"I appreciate that. Intellectually, I understand what's happening in my world, but I'm devastated emotionally. Here is this beautiful young man—intelligent, a gentleman, and the spitting image of Kai. If truth be told, I wish he was *our* son." Kate starts to tear up.

"You're still grieving the loss of your baby, Kate. And we all have to heal in our own way. If it consoles you, I intuitively feel you'll conceive when the time is right."

"Why do you think Noah came into our lives now?"

"I'm not sure. However, I feel the reason may present itself to you in time."

"I can't help but feel betrayed by Kai somehow. Yet I consciously know it isn't his fault. I feel so ashamed that I've been short with him since learning this news. It's like I can't control myself."

"Be gentle with yourself. Feel what you're feeling, but also, don't shut Kai out. He's an amazing, wonderful, and understanding man."

"I know." Kate starts to cry. "I think I'm jealous. I *am* jealous. I'm ashamed to feel this way, but *I* wanted to have *our* children, *our* family. Now this stranger comes and declares he's Kai's son, and I can see he is. He not only looks just like Kai, I think he'd be a son I'd be proud to claim as my own." Kate starts to sob again.

"Oh, honey." Olivia holds Kate tightly. "Go ahead, let it all come out."

Numb and still in disbelief, Kate returns home after visiting with Olivia, and all she can think to do is crawl under the covers. She has no energy for anything. Nevertheless, the four-hour respite does her good. She wakes to Kai moving about the master bedroom.

"Would you like to grab dinner in town?" asks Kai. "I was thinking about that new place, the Sea Cottage. I called and they have some open tables at six thirty."

"That would be nice. I've been hearing great things." Kate looks at the clock, which reads 5:30 p.m. "I'll get ready."

The Sea Cottage, a beautiful residential home transformed into a Zagat-rated restaurant, sits perched on a cliff in Princeville. Kai scored a lovely table out on the lanai with a spectacular view of the surrounding ocean and mountains.

"It's lovely," compliments Kate as she and Kai take their seats. She silently admires her handsome husband sitting across the table from her. Kai takes her hand, and her heart melts.

"I know Noah's news has been hard on you, Kate, and me too," says Kai.

"True. But Noah is innocent."

"I'm still processing. I'm not sure what it all means, how to relate."

A waiter presents the couple with menus, and they take a moment to peruse the fresh fare before ordering. The beautiful sunset on the horizon calms Kate and gives her balance.

"I read the latest issue of *Olivia!* on my break at work today," Kai says. "Your piece interviewing local farmers about their recipes using in-season produce was great. The photos were beautiful too."

"Mahalo."

"All going well with your other assignments?"

"Edward, my editor at *New York View*, asked me to do a piece on the top dining spots on Kauai's North Shore. I think I'm going to add this place to the list."

"How's the research on your mother's family tree coming?" Kai keeps their conversation light, refraining from delving more deeply. However, Kate's spirits rise when she talks about her work, and he loves that.

"I located some relatives, and I, um, was thinking I might like to take a trip to Taormina to meet with them. Weekend getaways, like the one we just took in Maui, are wonderful, but it's been over a year since our last real vacation. So what do you think about you and me going to Italy?"

"Summers are a busy time at the ER. I'll talk to the other doctors, though. Then I'll check the schedule and see when I can carve out some time." Kai reaches for Kate's hand and squeezes it tightly.

Moments later, the waiter brings them their dinners—grilled opah over a bed of lemony asparagus and jasmine rice. Kate and Kai eat in silence, each weighing how best to proceed with the topic of Noah.

"Kate, can we talk about Noah?" Kai asks about an hour later as they wait for their desserts. When Kate inhales deeply but doesn't respond, he continues, "I want to talk to you about your feelings and how you feel it best to proceed."

"I'm still processing," admits Kate. "The situation's a bit overwhelming. Noah said he'd like to get to know you . . . *us*. However, he's a grown man. I'm just wondering what that means. What do you think? Does Noah expect you to be his father? Me to be his stepmother?" Kate's emotions, which have become a mystery to her, start to rise, and again she feels like sobbing.

"The timing of this revelation is definitely not optimum." Kai places his hand over Kate's. "We're still grieving the loss of our baby, and then Noah presents himself. I'm not quite sure how to proceed either. Maybe just slowly. No expectations. Almost like meeting a new friend."

"Kai, I'm sorry." Kate simultaneously shakes her head and pulls her hand away, indicating she no longer wishes to share. "I can't talk about this anymore tonight. Okay? I just need more time to get my bearings. So, please, go ahead if you want to talk to or meet with Noah. That's fine. But I feel I'm coming unhinged, and it frightens me. So I really can't discuss it or take part right now."

"Okay. I understand."

Despite the elephant in the room looming, the rest of the dinner touches upon lighter conversation and laughter; for that, both Kate and Kai are grateful.

19

Over the next few weeks, Kate avoids any talk of Noah, and Kai is wise enough not to bring up the subject. Instead, he lets Noah know they need more time to process and discloses that he and Kate are still healing from the loss of their baby. Having just started medical school in Honolulu, Noah, concentrating on his studies, is understanding.

"I spoke to my partners about taking a vacation," Kai tells Kate one evening. "We looked at the schedule, and I can carve out about ten days next month if that works for you.

"Perfect. Sooner is better than later. Things are slow right now at the magazines. I've even told Olivia and Edward that I'll be able to check out article potentials while we're in Italy. That usually means part of the trip will be discounted."

Kai chuckles. "Wow. I'm impressed. What a mind. No grass grows under your feet."

"Would you be okay if I went ahead of time to do some work so I can be fully present when you join me?"

"Fine with me. That's a good plan, hon."

Kate instinctively knows that a change of scenery will do her good. A change of locale where she can be immersed in new surroundings and focus on her family research and work will help her stop overthinking and, with any luck, provide her with a fresh perspective. She aware that she's been testy and short tempered with Kai of late, which bothers her. She's screaming inside, trying to figure out what she feels, how to respond, and how to make this new piece—aka Noah—fit in their lives. The pressure of holding it together to appear "normal" is quite a task, and she's overwhelmed.

"Are you sure you don't want to talk to a counselor?" Olivia and Kate are taking a coffee break out on the lanai outside their office at Olivia's Princeville estate.

"I saw one after I miscarried, as you know. That helped me

realize that everyone has a personal time clock for healing. It was helpful talking to someone, but it got to be redundant. No one can take the pain away. Loss and grief are things we have to work through on a deep level for ourselves. There is no magic formula. Sorrow ebbs and flows, and I need to find my way through this."

"It's good that you recognize your pain and allow yourself to feel it."

"Sometimes, it just feels like a weight on my heart, and I find it hard to breathe."

"You know you can call me anytime you want to talk."

"I know. I read somewhere that delving deeper into my feelings and facing them—the grief, numbness, sorrow—and allowing all those emotions to happen until they pass . . . helps with healing. Self-care is vital as well."

"Like a facial, manicure, or massage . . . or shopping. I know that's my go-to."

Kate nods in agreement. "Retail therapy. It's good for the soul, but within reason. It can be so easy to go overboard and spend, or in my case, binge, on The Plumeria Café's double-double chocolate chunk or lemon-blueberry-coconut muffins."

"Honey, if that's your binge, you're a better person than me." Olivia laughs out loud.

"Usually, after an initial binge or two and some retail therapy, I get real about what I need to do for myself—*rest, eat right, and so on.* After that, I love being quiet and walking in nature or doing little things that make me feel better, like talking to God, praying, and spending quality time with friends and family," shares Kate. "Traveling to Taormina will be exciting, a new adventure. I need to escape right now."

"Well, it is stunningly beautiful there, and if you want help researching article potentials, I'm a phone call away."

"Really?"

"Well, the *Olivia!* show is on hiatus." Olivia takes another sip of her coffee.

"We discussed this a while back when we lunched at The Plumeria Café, you wanted us to 'percolate' on it, but I'd love it if you could join me."

"What about that needed alone time?"

"I'll be good after a few days alone doing what I need to with the family research. Then we could explore work ideas together before Kai joins me."

"Well . . . if we do that, then maybe I can get Grant to meet me the same time Kai arrives. That way, we can all play a bit and then go our separate ways to spend some romantic alone time with our mates like we did when the men joined us on our last trip to England."

"I like the sound of that!"

20

After talking to their significant others about a trip to Italy, and both husbands giving their thumbs up, Kate spends the next day plotting out her itinerary for the first leg of the journey when she'll be traveling solo. First, she locates a gorgeous clifftop resort perched overlooking the Ionian Sea. The venue, she reads on the website, was once the stately home of one of Italy's accomplished and respected families. Thanks to a commitment to write several articles featuring the hotel, a profile on *Olivia!* television show, and a call from Olivia's production team to negotiate advertising trades, the resort management has agreed to comp Kate and Kai's room and meals, as well as Olivia and Grant's, for their entire stay.

"I don't know how to thank you," gushes Kate as she hugs Olivia. "Both Kai and I are over the moon. What a gift."

"Hey, girlfriend, sometimes adding a little work to pleasure reaps major benefits."

"I feel so light and infused with new energy—and the possibilities."

"It's amazing how a change of scenery can inspire creativity and create positive energy."

"Taormina's history is so rich. I'm going to enjoy absorbing the area's beauty and culture."

"Have you located any relatives you might be able to connect with?"

"When my third-great-grandfather Leonardo Ricci immigrated to America, his sister, Sienna, remained in Sicily. I have cousins living in Taormina and Catania, primarily. So I'm working out some dates to get together with them when I visit."

For the remainder of the afternoon, Kate and Olivia map out article ideas for their trip to Italy. For starters they'll be arranging a few farm-to-table pictorials with the resort's head chef and several of the local restaurant favorites. Also on the schedule is a tour of top-rated wineries in the Mt. Etna region.

The rich volcanic soils and microclimates on the slopes near Italy's still-active volcano make a superb foundation for producing exceptional wines. The history and architecture of the region will also be full of article-worthy writeups, not to mention the eclectic local shops featuring all types of jewelry, art, colorful ceramics, clothing, and accessories. Kate also knows she'll be on the lookout for local art.

With every trip abroad or a vacation destination, Kate always relishes the idea of taking home representative artwork that reminds her of her travels.

"All this talk of meeting with chefs at the top local eateries, not to mention the thought of all that glorious Italian food, has made me hungry. Can I tempt you with more coffee and a blueberry scone?" asks Olivia.

"I've never met a scone I didn't like." The ladies laugh and head for Olivia's kitchen.

Later that night, home alone since Kai is working the late shift, Kate finds her mind drifting into dark territory after watching a commercial with a mother holding the cutest baby. Suddenly, that familiar feeling of sorrow envelops her. She takes a deep breath. To squelch the pain, and unconsciously looking to self-soothe, just like one of the living dead she follows a familiar instinct and heads toward the kitchen. Everything edible is fair game. The blueberry scone she brought home from Olivia's for Kai to enjoy sits under a glass dome on the kitchen counter—*bam!* She pulls out the remainder of the rice pudding she made last night—*gotcha!* Wait, there's a dark, 70 percent chocolate bar hidden in one of the fridge drawers. In feverish ecstasy, Kate mindlessly consumes two large squares of the rich, chocolatey goodness laden with almond clusters and coconut. Just as she is about to devour the third square, she stops dead in her tracks.

What are you doing? Why are you eating all this food? You had dinner less than an hour and a half ago!

Kate proceeds to ask herself questions, trying to get to the bottom of her food frenzy. There's some resistance. Finally, she puts two and two together. She was feeling great after a lovely meal and watching an uplifting movie. She remembers her mind started to go dark after the commercial. Her thoughts focus on the commercial's adorable, chubby little bundle. *Oh, I get it.* She realizes that's what caused her feelings of grief and utter sadness over the recent loss of her baby. She feels slightly ill now that she's stopped shoving food into her mouth, and her stomach feels distended. "That's what you get for pigging out," she yells aloud. "I know why you did that, Kate. However, it would be helpful to go into zombie mode and eat everything in your path. Got it?" The fact that Kate is talking to herself out loud makes her laugh.

Yeah, that's better. Okay, so I don't want food. I still need soothing. What will calm me down and make me feel better?

Kate heads for the master bedroom and turns on the light next to the bay window's seating area. As she does, she notices the book resting on the coffee table. It's a history and picture book of Sicily. She skims the pages, stops at the chapter on Taormina, and sits down to read.

Now we're talking.

"So then, they are no longer two but one flesh. Therefore what God has joined together, let not man separate."

~~Matthew 19:6

21

Annabella's Diary, 1868:

    It is before sunrise, but I can no longer sleep. Today my new life begins. I'm to be married to my sweetheart. My dear Papà will walk me down the aisle with all our relatives and friends bearing witness to our vows. Papà has been quite emotional this past week, constantly sharing memories and stories of me as a baby and young child—usually ending in wiping tears from his eyes. When Mamma sees this, she sighs, then kisses Papà on the cheek. And Mamma. Poor Mamma has fretted over every detail of the wedding celebration, which will take place in our villa's ballroom after the wedding ceremony at Chiesa di San Guiseppe in the Piazza IX Aprile.

    For the celebration dinner, round tables will be decorated with white linens and my family's beautiful silverware embellished with tiny rosebuds. The meal's courses will be served on the fine bone china decorated with chinoiserie decals and shiny gold rims. The gorgeous china is a wedding gift from one of my father's clients. Mamma has also arranged for each table to be decorated with beautiful plumeria centerpieces, my favorite flower.

    My fiancé's parents have given us the most wonderful Taormina villa as our wedding present. Stefano and I are so blessed.

    I heard that Giovanni, Regina, and Lorenzo could not come to the wedding. Instead, they are in Naples, tending to Regina's ill mother. I pray for them. I am also grateful that I am no longer being torn or dreaming about a man who cannot be mine. It was not easy to restrain my emotions, but praying to God and the Virgin Mary gave me strength and continues to give me much peace. I asked God to remove my burden, pain, and confusion, and He did. Now, I am to be married to a man who knows me and loves me deeply, makes me laugh, watches out for me, and I know he will be a wonderful husband and father. I truly understand the words of Psalms 106:1, Praise ye the LORD. O give thanks unto the LORD; for he is good: for his mercy endureth forever.

Annabella

"You look like a princess." Costanza Costa kisses her daughter's cheek as they stand, looking in the floor-length bedroom mirror. Annabella is dressed in a glorious, off-the-shoulder white satin and tulle wedding gown. The bodice, embellished with pearl beading, lace appliques, and a bell skirt, cinches at the waist and shows off her hourglass figure. The dress also boasts a modest train.

"Grazie, Mamma." Annabella smiles and adjusts her tiara as her mother smooths out her daughter's flowing veil.

"Come," orders Costanza lovingly. "We don't want to be late."

A gathering of birds in the Piazza IX Aprile, Taormina's main square, scatter and soar to the sky as Annabella's bridal carriage arrives at the Church of San Giuseppe. The magnificent structure, built during the seventeenth century, boasts a stunning stone façade in the baroque style. Oleander trees overflowing with fuchsia and white flowers and the scarlet bougainvillea, which drape over the piazza and church walls, create a glorious and colorful display.

Bells in the nearby twelfth-century clock tower ring as an escort in a dark suit and white waistcoat greets Annabella's carriage and helps guide the bride and her mother inside, where Anabella's father waits with the groom and their many guests.

The organ starts signaling the start of the wedding. Antonio takes his daughter's arm and proudly walks Annabella down the church's center aisle toward the altar, where Stefano waits.

Stefano is strikingly handsome in his wedding attire. His eyes radiate pure joy and love as he watches Annabella coming toward him. "My darling, you are so beautiful—inside and out," he whispers into Annabella's ear when she reaches his side. "I have longed for this day to make you my wife. *Ti amo.*"

"*Ti amo,*" replies Annabella with a smile.

The wedding celebration following the church ceremony takes place in the ballroom of the Villa Maria. The tables, so magnificently decorated, are further enhanced by floral arrangements of greenery and stunning plumeria blossoms that serve as runners down each table's center and in attractive floral centerpieces, creating a luxurious, garden-party feel.

A sea breeze rolls through the open ballroom doors that reveal a picture-perfect view of the terrace gardens decorated for the occasion.

"Costanza, my darling, the room is perfection." Antonio plants a kiss on his wife's hand as guests, a combination of Costa relatives, Stefano's relatives, and close friends and business associates, arrive.

"It's too bad that Giovanni, Regina, and Lorenzo couldn't celebrate with us today," laments Costanza. "Annabella was so close to Lorenzo. How is Regina's mother?"

"Not well, according to Giovanni. So they'll stay in Naples until there's a change in her health—for better or worse."

Later that evening, after the glorious wedding party, Annabella, in her private dressing room, prepares for her first evening of married life, while Stefano does the same. With a moment alone before her husband joins her, Annabella reflects on the day's events, some of which are a blur, but oh, so wonderful. She also reviews her life thus far, knowing she is embarking on a completely new chapter.

Her parents have given her so much. She's also grateful to Stefano's parents for the gift of living in this beautiful home in what she considers one of the most wonderful cities in the world. *Thank you, Father in Heaven, for my health, for all our relatives, and for Stefano.*

Annabella knows Stefano will be a wonderful husband. His devotion is sincere and constant. His engaging and witty personality make her laugh, and—not to forget—he is quite handsome.

So much has transpired over the months since she was first introduced to Giovanni. Annabella knows she and Giovanni did the right thing by not succumbing to their passion. It would have destroyed both their families. How could they live and thrive knowing they destroyed others' lives for the sake of their feelings, not to mention God's law? Giovanni committed to devoting his life to another.

Marriage vows should never be taken lightly, lest it loses their value and meaning. Annabella is well-read and worldly enough to know there will always be temptations in life, forces that cause discourse. How one handles them creates character and can also strengthen or destroy a marriage.

Nothing is more important than family, although it has pained her deeply to part from teaching Lorenzo and seeing Giovanni. Annabella rarely allows Giovanni to haunt her thoughts. Stefano is what's real, he is there for her, free to love her, and his love is solid, and with Stefano, she can build a respectable, beautiful life.

Annabella does feel desire for Stefano, and she knows their love will grow. And while she still doesn't fully comprehend her reaction to Giovanni, she has finally concluded that it was and must be God's will.

There may come a time when she doesn't wonder about Giovanni, but she knows that she must forgive and be gentle with herself, appreciating what she does have. Tonight, she looks forward with great anticipation and longing to be with what is natural and right—her loving husband, Stefano.

22

Hanalei, Kauai, Present Day

"After thinking more about my trip, I'm going to rearrange my flight to Italy." Kate sits on the Weke cottage's great room sofa, her computer in her lap, scrolling through airline flight listings. "I don't think I can handle twenty-four hours or more traveling straight from Kauai to Italy.

Flying from Kauai to New York and spending a day or so in Manhattan to do some in-person meetings at *New York View* would be the way to go, don't you think, hon?"

"Sure. That way you'll get a bit of a break and kill two birds with one stone," answers Kai. He is sprawled out on the coach next to her, reading his medical journal.

"Looks like I'll be able to fly from JFK to Rome and then to Sicily's Catania airport. The hotel in Taormina is about an hour's drive from where I land."

"Where will you stay in Manhattan for the layover?"

"Cindy and Vinnie offered me the use of their guest room." It has been quite a while since Kate has seen her dear friend Cindy, the *New York View* editor, and her husband Vinnie, and she remembers how luxurious their Midtown Manhattan townhome is, so Kate is definitely looking forward to spending time there.

"Well, that's an offer you don't want to refuse. Do you think you'll make it out to Long Island to visit with your sister, brother, and their families?" asks Kai, looking up from his journal. "Or maybe you and I could plan a few days' layover to visit them on our return trip from Europe via New York?"

"Now, that's a great idea! Summer's also a great time to visit Long Island."

Kai chuckles. "I have a bit of an ulterior motive. Your family loves boating as much as I do."

Kate continues to coordinate her travel plans and checks her incoming emails. "Kai!" Kate suddenly screams excitedly.

"What is it, babe?"

"A relative—Rosa De Luca, living in Taormina—sent me an email via the Generations site. She said she speaks perfect English and asks that I come to dinner when I'm in Taormina! She wants to put together a gathering of relatives."

"That's awesome, hon!"

"OMG! I'm so excited!" Kate gets up from her desk, jumping around, happy and lighthearted with the good news. She plops down on the couch next to Kai for some snuggle time to celebrate. Moments later, the mood is interrupted when Kai's cell phone rings.

It's Noah. The phone call is brief but manages to shift her amorous feelings from kissing to a craving for something cakey-sweet. She heads toward the kitchen, thinking about just the right edible to satisfy her desire.

Gotcha! Completely forgetting her recent vow not to act like a food-ravaged zombie to avoid intense feelings, Kate removes a plate of lemon bars from the fridge and places it on the kitchen counter. She frees a sizeable lemon square with a shaved coconut top from under its plastic wrap and moans when her teeth sink into the thick, tart, creamy bar.

"I thought the lemon squares were for your Nā Pīkake meeting tomorrow?" asks Kai, entering the kitchen after finishing the call with Noah.

Busted, thinks Kate, who mumbles a non sequitur while licking the last bit of yellow chiffon gooeyness and cakey crumbs from her fingers. Then, to avoid Kai's gaze, she turns away from him to wash her hands at the sink. "Is Noah in Kauai?"

"He's still at the university in Honolulu. He'll be on break soon and wants to plan a time to get together—maybe have lunch or dinner."

"Oh, that's nice. When will that be?" Kate tries to act nonchalant, although her stomach is churning with bubbling acid.

"Unfortunately, you'll be in Taormina. But I told him I could get together with him. Maybe we could also plan dinner for all three of us after the trip?"

Kate nods in agreement, feeling more than a little relieved that she has more time to process.

Standing with her back to Kai at the kitchen sink, she sighs deeply when Kai places his arms around her waist. He gently pushes her hair away from the back of her neck and starts to plant tender kisses on her neck and cheek. "Can we pick up where we left off?"

The warmth of Kai's breath and soft lips on Kate's neck and ears as his masculine hands glide gently across her back and the exposed skin of her arms begins to reignite Kate's desire. Then, when Kai tenderly probes her parted lips with his tongue, the world and all her concerns are put on hold.

"I'll miss you when you're in Europe." Kai reflects on how much he will miss his wife as he drives her to Lihue Airport several weeks later to catch her flight to Sicily by way of New York. "Do you realize this will be the longest time we've been apart since we became an official couple?"

"I'll miss you, too, hon. I'll call you as soon as I land at JFK."

"Let me know when you get to Cindy and Vinnie's, too." Kai reaches for Kate's hand, brings it to his lips, and kisses it. He continues holding her hand as he drives, releasing it only when necessary to park the car and help Kate unload and check her luggage.

"I'll be looking forward to you joining me in two weeks." Kate wraps her arms around Kai and squeezes. They kiss.

"Love you."

"Love you too."

Kai watches as Kate makes her way through check-in and disappears from view.

Leaving Kai behind, even with the full knowledge she'll see him soon, makes Kate emotional. She wipes a tear from her cheek but then takes a deep breath and heads to her departure gate.

Keep it together, Kate.

Once through the security check, Kate sits on a wooden bench in the airport's open-air courtyard and waiting room. Situated on hundreds of acres, Lihue Airport's one-level facility, which provides domestic, overseas, and inter-island carriers via eight gates, is welcoming, attractive, easy to navigate, and one of Kate's favorite airports.

Early as usual for the flight, Kate has some time to kill. She spies a nearby newsstand but opts out of a visit, noting that she has all the chewing gum, lozenges, power bars, snacks, and reading material she'll need for the flight. Besides, *Olivia!* magazine comped her first-class plane ticket, ensuring delivery of numerous snacks and a hot meal. Then, after the short layover at Los Angeles International Airport, the flight to New York's JFK airport will serve breakfast.

<h1 style="text-align:center">23</h1>

New York, Present Day

"Kate! Kate! Over here, girlfriend!" Cindy Maroni, Kate's East Coast-based BFF waves dramatically, making it impossible for Kate, standing with her luggage at New York's JFK baggage claim, not to notice.

Cindy, an attractive forty-something woman with a slightly chubby frame, is fashionably dressed in sleek black slacks and a white satin top with a string of pearls. As a fashion editor at the popular magazine, Cindy always dresses in suitable current and classic fashions. Her husband, Vinnie, Cindy's age, with a head of dark, wavy hair and a welcoming smile resembling the actor Vince Vaughn, is dressed in casual black Dockers and a crisp, buttoned-down, short-sleeved, blue cotton shirt. He also waves enthusiastically. The fact that everyone walking through baggage claim turns to look in Cindy and Vinnie's direction elicits a wave of laughter from Kate. She loves these two forever friends known for their big hearts, laughs, and fun times.

"Oh, how I've missed you both!" gushes Kate, kissing Vinnie's cheek.

"Let me take that monster." Vinnie reaches for the handle of Kate's large purple and white hibiscus-patterned suitcase on wheels.

"We've missed so much, girlfriend." Cindy crushes Kate with a bear hug. "Hey, you've lost some weight since I last squeezed you."

"Really? If I did, it's news to me. I've been eating up a storm lately."

"And me?" Cindy strikes a pose. "Notice anything different?" Cindy slowly twirls around, wiggling her hips and shaking her arms.

"You've lost weight?" responds Kate tentatively, knowing Cindy would be pleased, but while Cindy looks beautiful, any apparent weight loss is not yet noticeable.

"Yes. Ten pounds!"

"Yeah, she's lost weight alright," taunts Vinnie. "Now, instead of three squares daily, Cin eats five."

"You make that sound like I'm eating all day long," barks Cindy. She shoots Vinnie an exaggerated look and shakes her hand, threatening him with a playful swat to the shoulder.

"Experts say five small healthy meals a day spaced out helps with a person's metabolism," defends Kate.

Vinnie laughs. "Who said anything about *small*?"

"Hey!" This time Cindy does swat his shoulder.

"Babe, you know I'm only teasing."

Cindy rolls her eyes.

"You know I like a woman with a little meat on her bones. So come here, you sexy vixen, you." Vinnie pulls Cindy close for a smooch. "I love you, babe."

"Well, if that's the case, let's get back to Manhattan asap. I'm starving for dinner."

The trio burst out in laughter.

"Whaaat?" chuckles Cindy playfully. "You guys gotta problem with that?"

"Oh, how I missed you crazy, wild ones." Kate laughs and throws her arms around both friends.

Later that night, after dinner and trading in their street clothes for more comfortable attire, Kate and Cindy sit on the roof deck of Cindy and Vinny's uptown Manhattan townhome.

"I really like what you've done with this space, Cin," admires Kate, taking a sip of Chardonnay as she sinks back into the large, tropical-patterned cushions of the patio's cozy sofa. The deck, lushly appointed with potted plants in various shapes and sizes, and trees illuminated in strings of soft, white LED lighting, boasts a marvelous view of the sparkling city surrounding them.

"Well, after visiting you and Kai in Kauai, I was so inspired by your outdoor lanai and garden that I had to create a bit of city paradise for Vin and me." Cindy cuts a wedge of Brie from the charcuterie dessert plate that sits on the deck's wooden coffee table in front of them and generously lathers a whole wheat cracker with the creamy goodness before popping it into her mouth. "Okay, now that Vinnie left us to our girl talk," starts Cindy after choosing a small batch of plump violet grapes. "So, what's the latest with Noah?"

"Well . . . you know all there is to tell at this point," replies Kate after mentally reviewing everything that has transpired. Kate and Cindy make it a point to keep each other current with what's happening in their lives with almost daily calls, texts, and regular online Zoom sessions. "Noah will be visiting Kauai when he's on break from his studies, and Kai told me before I left for New York that he'll be meeting him for dinner."

"How do you feel about that?"

"To be honest, I'm not sure." Kate sighs. "Sometimes, I feel okay with it. Other times, I don't. I guess I'm just unsure how this will all play out. I wanted our family to be just me, Kai, and our children." She pauses, thinking. "Maybe I still have a big wound and residual issues about the miscarriage."

"I hear you, and I know how sad that was for you." Cindy reaches for her friend's hand and squeezes it. After Kate's miscarriage, Cindy read up on what *not* to say to her. Phrases like "It wasn't meant to be," "It's for the best," "Everything happens for a reason," "You'll have a child when the time is right," "I know how you feel," or "Something must have been wrong with the baby" are at the top of the NO list. Instead, the best response is to acknowledge the woman's loss and let them know you are sorry, listen, let them grieve, and offer practical support (i.e., bring them a meal or flowers, take them on an outing if they're game, or offer something you know they'll enjoy). So tonight, Cindy offers Kate an ear, and by touching Kate's hand, also offers friendship and support.

"I know Noah coming into our life isn't Kai's fault, but . . . to be honest, I'm harboring some resentment . . . and anger. I'm trying to work on forgiveness and acceptance, but it's just not happening in my heart. I also find myself snapping at unexpected moments."

"Snapping?" asks Cindy.

"Being short with Kai, crying for no apparent reason, feeling— oh, just, I don't know."

"Do you think talking to a professional again might help?"

"I can call anytime I need another appointment. I've realized, though, that I need to process and heal differently. Hearing myself repeat the same sentiments doesn't cut it for me," continues Kate as the ladies look out over the city, sipping their drinks. "I'm glad I'm going to Italy before I meet up with Olivia and Kai. I'm looking forward to some alone time to think and process without distractions."

"Sounds fabulous. Taking some time off from my day-to-day always helps me with perspective." Cindy pops another grape into her mouth. "I'm so glad you decided to layover in New York for a few days."

"I couldn't fly into JFK and not spend some time with you or Vin . . . or not go in and see Ed at *New York View*.

"Ed told me he insists on taking us to lunch tomorrow. He wants to try out Wild Fig, a new place in Midtown."

"Oh, I've heard of that. Wild Fig has great vegan dishes."

"Really? Yuck." Cindy sticks out her tongue in disgust.

"They also have other choices—you know, regular people's food," says Kate offhandedly.

"Regular people's food. Hmmm. Is that what I am? A regular-people food eater?" Cindy laughs out loud.

"You know what I mean."

"Oh, you mean regular people eat food like quarter-pound beef burgers with lots of cheese, steak and potatoes, BBQ baby back ribs, onion rings, and—"

"I wouldn't go that far."

"Not to worry. I checked the menu online to guarantee there's *something* on the menu I can eat, and the restaurant has more than just garden vegetables."

"What a relief," Kate mocks before switching the subject. "Ed is such a great guy. He's been so good about me working remotely."

"He's the best boss ever," agrees Cindy. "Working for both *Olivia* and *New York View* has worked well for you."

"I feel very blessed in that regard."

"Will you be seeing your brother and sister on this trip?"

"Carla and Derek, along with my sister-in-law and brother-in-law, will come to Manhattan to meet me for dinner tomorrow. Kai and I plan to visit the rest of the family on Long Island on a layover when we fly back from Italy. Hey, would you and Vinnie want to join us tomorrow? I know they'd love to see you two. You are family, you know?"

"Well, only if there will be *regular people's food*."

Both ladies laugh out loud.

*"Fill your paper with the breathings
of your heart."*

~~William Wordsworth

24

The next day, Kate makes her way down the corridors of *New York View's* stylish Madison Avenue digs, often stopping in an office here and there to say hello to a colleague. Finally, she makes her way to the office of her editor and publisher, Edward Alexander.

"Aloha, Kate!" Edward, a strikingly handsome, charismatic man of sixty-eight with a commanding presence and kind demeanor, walks from behind his massive mahogany desk to hug Kate. "You look fantastic."

"So do you," replies Kate. Edward's head of thick silver hair, athletic physique, and steel blue eyes reveal the passion and demeanor of a much younger man. A sophisticated, cultured, self-made man and devoted husband and father, Edward Alexander has been like a second father to Kate, shepherding her from a novice just out of journalism school to the award-winning writer she is now. When Kate thought she might have to resign from the magazine after her engagement to Kai, Edward was only too keen to give a thumbs up to the idea of Kate working as a freelance contributor from Kauai.

Kate takes a seat in the plush, burgundy leather chair facing Edward's desk. Her eyes wander to several of Edward's family photos sitting on his desk—the Alexander family smiling on one of their various European vacations, relaxing on the glistening beaches of Fiji, and sailing their yacht in the Peconic Bay.

"Can I get you something to drink? Coffee? Naturally-flavored cranberry-orange or water?"

"Cranberry-orange would be perfect," replies Kate as Edward heads to his office beverage station. "I notice you've got a few more sailing awards on your shelves," she says, reviewing the beautiful custom-made wooden bookshelves filled with antique finds and first-edition books that line the office

"Yup. You know me and sailing. The kids have caught the bug too."

"Really?

"Jared and James can't get enough, and they're on their boat

111

every good-weather weekend. Even their sister, Elizabeth, is taking lessons." Edward hands Kate a silver, double-sided photo—shots of his children on a boat on the left and, on the right, his beautiful wife, Meredith.

"They're gorgeous. What fun."

"That they are." Edward grins before changing the subject. "I know Hawaii and Kai are treating you well. Excited to be headed to Italy?"

"What do you think?"

Edward laughs. He knows Kate is ecstatic. "Well, I'm pleased you'll be doing a few pieces for *New York View*. What's on your schedule?"

"Well, you know me and food. I was thinking about an article on some of Sicily's more unique foods and how they're created."

Edward laughs. "Of course you'll have to do some firsthand research."

"Of course."

"I was thinking it might be fun for you to do a personal account, maybe a walking tour, of some favorite spots—restaurants, galleries, the architecture, fun things-to-do. And maybe a piece on the lifestyle, comparing it to how we live in the States."

"I love it. I was also thinking about coordinating some interviews with opera singers. Taormina has a very picturesque theatre where professionals perform beloved Italian operas."

"Like Giuseppe Verdi's *La Traviata* and Puccini's *Madame Butterfly*?"

"Exactly. I'll put together a list of other ideas and email them to you once I get there and have a chance to check things out."

"I have the ad department talking with some of our travel and hospitality advertisers to see how we might network for the articles. I'll keep you posted should they want you to cover something specific. I'm also going to have the photo department coordinate with a local, English-speaking photographer you can work with."

Kate smiles broadly. Edward always plans the best for her.

"Are you hungry?" When Kate nods, Edward stands up, and Kate follows his lead. "Come one, then. Let's talk over other ideas at lunch. I'm famished."

"What a great lunch this afternoon with Edward and dinner tonight with the family," remarks Kate, back at Cindy and Vinnie's townhome, removing the last of her makeup. Kate and her sister Carla are both in their PJs, and Carla sits on one of the guest room's two twin beds, watching Kate in the en suite bathroom. "It was so good to see the family, and I'm happy you were able to stay with me tonight."

"Me staying here tonight will give my husband and son some bonding time. Besides, I wanted to have some sister time."

"I'm glad we do our weekly Zooms, but it's so good to see you in person." Kate walks over and hugs her sister.

"Are you guys decent?" shouts Cindy, knocking on the closed bedroom door.

"Come on in, Cin," calls Kate.

"I just wanted to see if you have everything you need," says Cindy, dressed in a flowing, floral silk bathrobe.

Kate looks at Carla, who nods, and she turns to Cindy. "Yup."

"Gee, Cin, even at night, you're glam. Love the robe," says Carla.

"Well, *daahling*, I have to maintain my image, now don't I?" responds Cindy, raising her arms, palms turned out, and speaking with an upper-class British accent. "Shall I leave you two guys alone?" she continues. From her tone of voice and expression, it's clear she is secretly hoping they want her to stay.

"Stay," answers Kate.

"You're a sister too." Carla pats the bed for Cindy to sit on.

"Awesome. I was hoping you'd say that." Cindy sits beside Carla. "Okay, now who do we want to dis?"

Carla and Kate laugh.

"Oh, almost forgot!" Cindy jumps up. "I have something for you, Kate. Be right back."

"Oh, yeah, I have something for you too," says Carla. "You're going to love this!" She digs into her overnight bag and pulls out a dark-red, velvet-bound book kept shut by a gold clasp.

"What's that?"

"It's a diary. The entry dates start from 1868 and go to the 1930s."

"Whose is it?" Sitting on the bed next to Carla, Kate looks at the first pages of the journal. "Here." Kate points, recognizing Annabella's name. "Our maternal fourth-great-grandmother."

"The journal's written in Italian, though."

"Where did you get it?" asks Kate.

"After Mom passed I took some boxes from their basement to sort through them and found the diary. Since you're researching the family tree, I thought you might find it interesting."

"I do." Kate nods, flipping through the delicate journal pages. "Gee, I wish I knew Italian. Do we know anyone who reads Italian?"

"Well, when our third-great-grandpa Leonardo came to America in the early 1900s, he and many other immigrants wanted to assimilate. But unfortunately, that sometimes included not teaching their descendants their native tongue. So no one in our family, that's for sure," says Carla.

"I wonder how Mom ended up with the diary. Annabella lived in Italy."

"The diary entries go to the 1930s. I remember hearing that Annabella visited her family in Boston at some point. Maybe she left the diary," Carla suggests.

"Maybe." Kate sighs. "Do you mind if I take it with me to Italy? I'd love to show it to our relative Rosa. Maybe she can translate some entries for me."

"That's why I wanted to give it to you."

"Thanks, Sis."

Moments later, Cindy dashes back into the room and dramatically presents Kate with a large gift bag with attractive script lettering that reads Amore in the middle of a sea of pretty flowers. "For you. Amore!" announces Cindy, handing Kate the bag. "*Viva Italia!*"

Carefully pulling aside layers of pink tissue paper, Kate gushes when she sees a stunning, oversized, cognac-colored leather tote with braided straps and embossed with flowers. "OMG!"

"Wow!" Carla says admiringly.

"It's made in Italy—genuine Italian leather!" yells Cindy, as excited as Kate.

"It's just gorgeous! And big enough to hold my laptop, datebook, and more." Kate grabs Cindy and gives her a bear hug. "I love, love, love it! Thank you."

"What's that?" Cindy spies the red velvet diary.

"Carla found it in one of the boxes she was sorting through after Dad sold the family home," answers Kate.

"It appears to be our maternal fourth-great-grandmother's."

"Oooh. Does it have anything juicy? Diaries usually do." Cindy rubs her palms together in anticipation.

Kate chuckles. "Don't get too excited. It's written in Italian."

"Boo-hoo." Cindy pretends to pout and makes a sad face.

"I'll keep you apprised on anything I learn that *isn't fit to print*." The ladies laugh.

"Now that's my girl." Cindy gives Kate a thumbs up.

"How are you feeling, Sis?" asks Carla the following day after she, Kate, and Cindy spent the night chatting until the wee hours of the morning.

"I'll be good to go after another cup of coffee." Kate chuckles as she tops off her mug with coffee from the stainless-steel thermal carafe resting on Cindy's kitchen table. The ladies, still in their PJs, are eating a hardy breakfast of scrambled eggs, bagels, and fruit salad.

"Getting excited about leaving tonight?" asks Carla."

"Will you be able to sleep on the plane?" asks Cindy.

Kate laughs. "Sure, I can sleep anywhere. I'll get to Rome early afternoon, then fly to Catania after a short layover if all goes well. The flight from Rome to Catania is a little over an hour. Then it's about another fifty minutes or so by car to where I'm staying in Taormina."

"Yikes. I hope you won't be toast," comments Cindy, pouring herself another cup of coffee.

"To avoid jetlag, the rule of thumb is to go to bed at your normal time in the city you're visiting. Moving around will keep me occupied, so I'm going to try and stay up until nine thirty or ten p.m. if I can."

"I have your itinerary and the hotel info, but do us a favor, Sis. Group text us when you've arrived safely in Italy, and then again when you get to your hotel in Taormina," Carla requests.

Chewing on a bagel slathered with cream cheese and slices of smoked salmon, Kate nods agreement.

"And do me another favor, Sis," says Cindy playfully. "Shoot me some pics of some hot Italian delicacies."

"Parmigiana? Risotto? Cannoli? Gelato?" Kate fires the list of well-loved Italian classics in rapid succession."

Cindy pauses dramatically and thinks. "I was referring more to the tall, dark, handsome kind . . . but sure, that too."

The ladies howl with laughter.

"Were a man to spend only one day in Sicily
and ask, 'What must one see?' I would
answer him without hesitation, 'Taormina."
It is only a landscape, but a landscape where
you find everything on earth that seems
made to seduce the eyes, the mind,
and the imagination."

~~Guy de Maupassant

25

———

Grateful to be traveling to Italy first class courtesy of her magazine employers—*Olivia!* and *New York View*—Kate removes her flats and sinks into her luxurious seat after a smooth takeoff. To get her into a more-relaxed mood, she watches two uplifting, romantic comedies set in Italy—*Only You* and *Letters to Juliet*. During movie time, a delicious lobster-risotto dinner is served with a classic Caesar salad and a basket of rosemary focaccia. For dessert Kate finds it impossible to say no to a mouth-watering tiramisu. Eating every delightful morsel, she rationalizes that she'll work off the calories walking the picturesque streets of Taormina.

Soon after her meal, the movies, and partaking of a glass of Chardonnay that the flight attendant kept refreshing, Kate's eyes start to feel like rocks. Still not yet ready for slumber, she flips on her seat's reading light and pulls out the mystery novel she picked up at one of JFK's airport gift stores. After several minutes of reading, her eyes refuse to focus or stay open. Reclining her seat into its full sleeping position, Kate places her seat's pillow under her head and, wrapping her body with the soft blanket provided, falls quickly into a deep slumber.

Approximately four hours later, Kate wakes to the clattering of dishes in the steward's galley kitchen, where flight attendants are preparing a continental breakfast for the first-class passengers. Kate puts her seat in an upright position in anticipation. "Excuse me, sir, how much longer until we land in Rome?" she asks as an attendant offers her coffee.

"About an hour and a half, Miss."

"Please," she replies, acknowledging the offer of coffee. "No sugar, just cream." Kate also orders a fruit bowl and a warm demi-baguette which she lathers in Brie cheese.

As the plane descends slowly toward the earth for its

subsequent landing at Rome's Leonardo da Vinci International Airport, Kate notices a mixture of old and new architecture in this almost 3,000-year-old city. Excited and full of anticipation, she keeps her eyes glued to her seat window to luxuriate in and record the magnificent views of Rome from the clouds with her iPhone. Finally, passenger applause erupts when the plane's wheels hit the tarmac in a smooth landing.

Rome, Italy

Located in the pretty seaside town of Fiumicino, twenty miles southwest of Rome's center, the Leonardo da Vinci Airport, a modern facility covering a little over six square miles, is bustling with international travelers. As soon as Kate bids the attendants farewell, she makes her way to the flight information display to check on her connecting flight to Catania. With about an hour's layover, she has time to walk the elegant airport halls. Listening to a cacophony of languages is the only indicator that she is in Europe. The airport looks like any other she might see in a metropolitan city.

Perusing the duty-free shops, Kate spritzes herself with a few of the latest designer perfumes and checks her makeup and attire in one of the store's floor-to-ceiling mirrors. To kill a bit more time before heading to her plane's assigned gate, she visits an airport newsstand and picks up sugar-free chewing gum and a large bottle each of blood orange and black raspberry sparkling San Pellegrino.

"Grazie," says Kate, thanking the cashier in Italian before heading to her gate.

Catania, Italy

Kate boards a much smaller plane than the massive Airbus she flew in from JFK to Rome. The semi-full flight leaves on time and arrives at Catania-Fontanarossa Airport (also known as Vincenzo Bellini Airport after the Catania-born opera composer) five minutes earlier than its scheduled arrival time.

Making her way toward baggage claim, Kate notices that although smaller than the airport in Rome, the Catania airport is just as lively.

As she retrieves her luggage from the baggage carousel, she spies a jovial man of about sixty wearing a beret, a white shirt with the sleeves rolled up, and black pants, walking through the crowd. He holds a sign with her name spelled out in large letters in black magic marker. Kate waves to him.

"*Buona sera*, Signorina," greets the driver. "My name"—the man holds his hand across his chest—"Bruno. *Seguimi*. Follow me," he orders after Kate introduces herself. He takes one of Kate's suitcases in each hand and begins heading toward the airport exit.

Kate is exceedingly grateful that she took Kai's advice and prebooked her taxi from the airport to Taormina before she left for Italy. Navigating her way around the airport and not knowing much Italian might have been problematic.

Once inside Bruno's comfortable van, Kate relaxes and keeps her eyes glued to her window as they travel from the airport to the coast. Catania, Sicily's second-largest city, sits under the shade of the majestic, still-active volcano Mount Etna and beside the magnificent crystal waters of the Ionian Sea. The town, filled with charm and personality, boasts stunning Baroque architecture featured in elegant palaces, beautiful churches with unique adornments, and Greek and Roman ruins. The streets are full of pink and fuchsia oleander and bougainvillea in bloom.

"Is that plumeria?" asks Kate, thrilled to see her favorite tree.

Bruno looks in his rearview mirror and nods. "*Si, pomelia*."

Pomelia. Kate looks up the word on her phone and learns that *pomelia* is also known as *plumeria* and *frangipani*. Sicilian women used to give it to their daughters (or granddaughters) after marriage to adorn their new home, which is why the flower acquired a deep-meaning bond to a sense of familiar affection and heritage. Kate can relate.

Looking out at unobstructed views of the exquisite turquoise-colored Ionian Sea, Kate taps the control button on her armrest to lower the car's window to breathe in the fresh ocean air. She read before her trip that the ocean's unique color in this part of the world is partly due to the reflection of the blue skies. Additionally, the lack of nutrients in the water leads to the inhibition of algae growth, which makes the

Mediterranean clear and better able to absorb/scatter sunlight, thus making the sea appear a vibrant blue.

As they travel the hilly terrain and grow closer to Taormina, Kate notices many homesteads surrounded by lava-rock walls and lush, green vegetation. There are also rows of old stone buildings in pleasing patinas and plaster adornments with magnificent carved-wood doors. They pass through picturesque tiny villages with houses planted in straight rows and areas of expansive farmland as far as the eye can see. At every twist and turn of the road, Kate eagerly uses her camera to capture images that speak to her.

As the van continues to climb, Kate can once again view the ocean to her right and, on the left, estates tucked into the rocky hillside. Finally, they arrive at Villa Bella Vista.

Taormina, Province of Messina, Italy, Present Day

The hotel's attractive, pastel-lemon stone façade faces the ocean. White stone casings accent the doors and windows, and the villa's backdrop against lushly planted grounds and greenery paints an idyllic picture.

"*Bellissima!*" declares Bruno, turning around to look at Kate in the back seat. He gives her the universal thumbs up to signify "Well done."

"Grazie." Kate chuckles and returns the thumbs up, then signs the sales receipt for her ride. She makes sure to tip Bruno well. He was an excellent driver who did his best to point out local attractions.

"My card." Bruno hands Kate his business card. "Need ride. *Telefono* Bruno. *Si?*"

"Si," replies Kate accepting the card. Bruno moves to the back of the van to retrieve Kate's luggage for the approaching hotel porters.

"*Buona serata.*" Bruno tips his hat, leaving Kate at the villa's front entrance.

"Grazie," Kate calls one last time as she waves goodbye then follows the bellman to the entrance of the hotel. Her mouth drops in awe, and she stands transfixed as she scans the stunningly elegant lobby of this luxury, five-star hotel. It had once been a Dominican monastery and the decor is breathtaking. Done in soothing whites and beige hues, with red, yellow, teal, and blue accents, ornate gold fixtures, cathedral ceilings, gleaming parquet wood floors, and white paneled walls with attractive wood molding, strategically placed classical paintings, and ornate gold chandeliers, the hotel is a remodeled wonder resembling more a high-end modern palace than one would expect from a centuries-old monastery. The floor-to-ceiling windows showcase breathtaking panoramic views of Taormina Bay and Mount Etna.

I understand why Olivia booked this hotel and why it's become a hub for famous writers, painters, and composers.

Immediately, Kate can feel her creative juices flow with inspiration. She imagines herself sitting on her suite's balcony, typing away on her laptop as the breezes roll off the blue waters and up to her terrace. She pictures herself pausing to sip her cappuccino, breathe in the fragrant plumeria, and enjoy the exotic historical views. *Heaven.*

"Buona serata, Signorina." A smiling hotel concierge greets Kate. The attractive fifty-something, silver-haired clerk, wearing a cream-colored jacket, white shirt, and light blue patterned tie, stands behind a long, white marble check-in counter. Next to where he stands is a colorful display of beautiful tropical flowers overflowing a large terracotta urn strategically placed to welcome guests.

"Grazie," replies Kate. Then she checks her phone app to translate her next words from English to Italian. "*Lei parla inglese?*"

"I speak English, Mrs. Stevens. Welcome to Villa Bella Vista."

After the check-in, Kate follows a bellman pushing a brass trolley filled with her belongings through the lobby.

The beautiful change of scenery is quickly having a healing effect that's transportive. Already she can feel her demeanor altering. Kate breathes deeply, almost wanting to pinch herself for her good fortune in making this magnificent retreat her home for the next few weeks.

"Oh, my," she whispers as she enters the living room of the massive two-bedroom suite. A wall of French doors with a terrace just beyond frames a sweeping view of the coast. Like the lobby, ornate molding adorns the suite's high ceilings, and the room is elegantly appointed in soothing, creamy-white tones accented with touches of aqua, yellow, green, and red. A kitchen and dining table sit opposite a large sofa and seating area. The feel is glamorous, calming, and sublime.

After Kate tips the bellman and he exits, she explores the suite. Each master bedroom is a duplicate of the other, offering a king-size bed, a private seating area with a sofa and writing desk, and an oversized bathroom with a sunken, jetted tub, double sinks, a walk-in shower, and makeup vanity and chair. The French doors in each suite lead out to private garden terraces with awe-inspiring views.

Glancing at the four o'clock time on her phone, Kate knows it's four a.m. Hawaii time, so she chooses to email rather than text Kai, her father, and Olivia that she's arrived at her hotel. She also adds a few photos of the suite and its amazing views. Next, as it's ten a.m. in New York, Kate alerts her sister and Cindy that she has arrived. Almost immediately, Cindy rings Kate on FaceTime.

"OMG!" screams Cindy into her phone screen. She's still dressed in her PJs, with no makeup and her hair piled high on her head.

"Buongiorno, *amico mio*," Kate replies with a chuckle. "You look adorable with your hair like that."

"Oh, yeah, just divine." Cindy snickers before she screams with delight again. "Show me around your Italian digs, *per favore*."

"Sure." Kate takes her around the suite, then onto the private garden terrace to show her the unobstructed view.

"Killer. Aren't you glad the room is a travel comp? I can't imagine what a room like that costs."

Kate laughs. "*Molto denaro*, I'm sure. I'm still pinching myself. But hey, Cin, look at my writing desk and the view. Although I can also write on the terrace."

"Um, excuse me, but . . . writing? Don't you want to go exploring?"

"There'll be time for that. I feel so inspired. I want to work on my novel. When Olivia arrives, we'll be researching story ideas and setting them up."

"Well, then go for it, girl."

When the FaceTime call with Cindy ends, Kate unpacks and then makes a dinner reservation for 7:30 p.m. on the hotel dining room terrace. This way, she'll have time to relax, wash off the travel, and tend to a few things. Eating a bit later than usual will also force her to stay awake until her regular bedtime, thus limiting the jet lag she may feel the next day.

Accustomed to showering most days, luxuriating in the massive, jetted tub is a treat. To make the experience more memorable, Kate dumps a good portion of bath gel into the steamy water and is pleased with the abundance of bubbles it creates. Before jumping in, she feasts on some dried apricots and assorted nuts from the welcome basket and uncorks a bottle of award-winning Pinot Grigio.

Mmm. Kate smells the wine's bouquet as she swishes it around a long-stemmed, crystal glass she took from the room's bar. *Delightful.* As she walks toward the bath, she gingerly sips, then places her glass on the tub's big marble ledge.

"Aaaah," sighs Kate audibly as she submerges herself in the comforting, foamy warmth of the tub. Leaning back onto the towel she's rolled up into a pillow and propped behind her head, all the tension in her body dissipates. She drifts into a delightful alpha state for the next thirty minutes, only coming back to earth when her stomach rouses her in hunger.

Slipping into a simple scoop-necked, sleeveless, flowing black Boho midi dress and wedge sandals, Kate applies a light dusting of makeup. She compliments her outfit by putting on a long, silver, Sedona-style turquoise pendant with matching turquoise earrings before heading to dinner.

Round patio tables draped in white linens, each table featuring a vase of colorful flowers, are placed around the charming hotel dining room's stone terrace. Tiny, twinkling white candles in clear glass holders provide soft, atmospheric lighting.

Kate is shown to a table with a perfect view of the evening's sky, which is starting to turn pinky-purple over the blue sea. The waiter pours a glass of San Pelligrino and allows Kate to review the menu. Famished, it doesn't take her long to order a lemon-arugula salad tossed in a lemon vinaigrette with shaved Parmesan cheese and served with rosemary crostini to start. For her main course, Kate chooses pasta alla Norma, a traditional Sicilian dish combining pasta and sautéed eggplant in a tomato sauce topped with Ricotta Salata cheese.

Halfway through her entrée, Kate gets a FaceTime call. It's Kai. After they both exchange greetings, Kate says, "I'm sitting by my lonesome, enjoying a fantastic meal and overlooking a moonlit ocean."

"Show me."

Kate turns her phone around to show Kai her view. "It's so romantic here. I miss you." Kate pouts playfully. "You look so yummy in your T-shirt and shorts."

Kai chuckles and blows Kate a kiss. "Miss you too, hon. But we'll be together real soon. In the meantime, I'll be thinking of you. Keep me posted on the family outreach."

"Will do. I want to settle in tonight and get a good night's sleep, so I'll call Rosa tomorrow. I'm starting to feel like I'm going to lift out of my body, I'm so tired."

"Okay, sweetie. I'll let you go. Love you. Send me photos of everything."

Back in her suite and readying for bed, Kate's thoughts return to Kai. Oh, how she misses him. Being this far away, she can forget Noah, the elephant in the room. When her thoughts travel to the topic and reality of Noah, she finds that her body gets tense, and her anger starts to rise.

No, don't go there. Don't obsess.

Kate quickly pushes any unsettling thoughts out of her mind and opts to lose herself in a best-selling mystery novel that she packed. Her eyelids feel like two-ton rocks as she struggles to read in bed. She turns to the clock on her nightstand. It's 9:30 p.m. If only she could stay awake at least another hour. She tries to push through her tiredness and read on; however, it's no use. She sets her book on the nightstand, turns off the table light, and is out cold in seconds.

In her dream, Kate holds a beautiful baby. As Kate smiles, making eye contact, the infant smiles joyfully, wiggling with pleasure, its little hand reaching to grasp a finger on Kate's hand. Kate's heart bursts with love. In the next instant, Kate is walking alone down a dirt road with tall greenery on either side. While the scene is beautiful, she is aware of her despair and longing to have the child in her arms again. Suddenly, in front of her and walking toward her, is Kai and, beside him, another man. The other man walks with his head down. Kate can't see his face. When he looks up, she sees it is Noah.

"Huh!" gasps Kate, waking with a start. Rays of light slip in between an opening in the floor-to-ceiling drapes, revealing a sunny day. Kate takes a moment to get her bearings, then quickly pushes the dream from her consciousness and picks up the hotel phone to order breakfast.

Rising from the bed, Kate heads for her room's desk and powers up her laptop. Her nightwear—an attractive, long, jersey nightgown in a floral pattern that looks more like evening attire than sleepwear—makes it so that she does not need to wear a robe. Browsing through her inbox, Kate responds to Olivia's email asking her to send more photos of the hotel and room. Kate promptly obliges. She also answers emails from her father and siblings. Then there's a knock at the door.

Room service—a pot of black coffee, a small carafe of unsweetened almond milk, a fruit bowl, and a toasted baguette with butter—is laid out for her on the room's terrace. Kate brings her laptop as her breakfast companion.

Sorting through other correspondence between sips of coffee, she finds a new email from her newly found relative Rosa, who invites Kate to dinner the following evening. Rosa lets Kate know she has contacted other family members to attend and even arranged for her grandson to pick up Kate at the hotel. After emailing Rosa a thank you, Kate eats her breakfast and ponders everything that awaits her on her first full day in this Italian paradise.

"*Family and friends are hidden treasures,
seek them out and enjoy their riches.*

~~Wanda Hope Carter

26

After breakfast, Kate rents a luxury brand, two-wheeled electric scooter known as a Vespa, a popular mode of transportation in Italy, from the hotel's on-site supply for guests. Next, she makes her way to the Piazza IX Aprile. Populated with beautiful buildings, monuments, shops, and restaurants, where, from its terrace, amazing views of Mt. Etna, the Bay of Naxos, and the ancient theatre of Taormina—the Teatro Greco—are visible, the piazza is Taormina's main square and gathering place. The piazza only allows foot traffic, so Kate parks her Vespa adjacent to the main square. Her first stop is the Church of San Giuseppe. Built during the seventeenth century, the church is a gorgeous example of Sicilian Baroque architecture. Adjacent is a clock tower, Torre dell'Orologio, rebuilt and restored many times since its first incarnation in the twelfth century.

Rich in history and beauty, and with a landscape very different from home, Kate becomes keenly aware of the world's expansiveness. The melodic sounds of the spoken Italian language, mixed with a spattering of French, German, and other tongues, surround her. The aromatic scent of the square's restaurants—a potpourri of garlic, tomato, herbs, fresh fish on the grill, and baking bread—fills the air.

Couples laugh and converse as they dine under umbrellas in the outdoor cafes, a quartet of musicians plays soothing sounds, visions of young lovers holding hands and kissing, and little children playing by the fountain are proof that the square is teeming with life and love. The scene touches Kate profoundly. She gulps, instantly tearing up and quickly wiping the wetness out from under her sunglasses, not wanting anyone to notice.

Local painters catch Kate's attention next. The artists sit in a little group, sketching and painting various picturesque scenes as passersby watch them create and sell their works. Then one image grabs Kate's eye. It's a pretty watercolor capturing a charming outdoor café drenched in golden light. The beautiful foliage surrounding the café and the view of the crystal ocean where stone structures protrude from the jagged cliffs make it a perfect image for Kate to remember this moment. Noting that the painting is an ideal size, an 8 x 10 she can easily fit into her oversize leather satchel, she pays the artist's asking price, and her purchase is wrapped securely with protective wrapping for safekeeping.

Next, Kate visits the Church of San Giuseppe and lights a candle. She prays for Kai, her family, and her friends. For herself, she asks for divine guidance, understanding, and peace.

After leaving the church, Kate looks at her phone, longing to connect with Kai. 12:30 pm. Kai's probably sound asleep. Kate texts him anyway.

Thinking of you. I miss you, my love. XO.

Kate starts to tear up again. Seconds later, she receives a text from Kai.

Hon, I love and miss you, too. Want to FaceTime?

Kate replies immediately.

Yes!

Seconds later, face to face with her love, she starts to cry.

"Oh, hon. I miss you too." Kai's voice is calm and soothing.

"I don't know why I'm so emotional," comments Kate, wiping the tears from her cheeks. She takes a deep breath for balance. "There, I'm better now."

"We'll be together soon," Kai reassures her. "When will you be meeting Rosa?"

"Tomorrow for dinner. Rosa arranged for a gathering of relatives at her home. She's sending her grandson to pick me up."

"Good. So you'll be with family tomorrow. Olivia will be there shortly as well."

"I've traveled by myself many times. But, I, I, well . . . I don't know what came over me today. I'm okay now, though, hon."

"You sure?"

"Yes."

"No matter what, let's check in every night. Want to say nine p.m. Kauai time, that's nine a.m. your time?"

"Sure."

"And we'll text in between."

"I love you."

"I love you too, sweetheart."

Feeling much better after talking to Kai, Kate decides to grab a bite at one of the local outdoor patio cafés. She picks a quiet table with an ocean view, orders, then reviews her emotions.

I'm not PMSing at this time of the month. Could it be seeing the children? The young, happy families and mothers with their babies?

Kate starts to tear up again.

Okay, then. I guess that's it. Unresolved pain from losing the baby, from holding in anger about Noah, feeling distant from Kai. Why can't I just let it go?

Kate has read many books on healing and one especially struck her. Swiss-American psychiatrist Elisabeth Kübler-Ross in her 1969 book, *On Death and Dying*, examined five of the most common emotional reactions to losing someone. Her five-stages-of-grief theory includes denial, anger, bargaining, depression, and acceptance. And although healing from loss is a personal journey, there's no blueprint for getting over a loss.

Kate knows she keeps going in and out of the denial stage. Sometimes, a person denies what happens or feels they cannot survive—becoming numb, aware of, but ignoring the loss, pretending things will all be okay, dealing with anything but the actual reality. Likewise, although Kate has felt anger and has never gone into the bargaining stage, she has gone in and out of depression—feeling lethargic, sleeping more than the norm, distracted, vulnerable, and unable to focus, eating more than usual or not enough.

While Kate feels she's reached the stage of acceptance—that she miscarried but will be okay—that doesn't mean there won't be any "bad" days. If she digs down, she also knows she hasn't entirely accepted the reality of Noah—or what that will mean for her and Kai's future. Truth be told, Kate had quite a different idea of what her and Kai's future would be, so coming to terms with the loss of their child, and accepting Noah, are things that still need to be processed.

After lunch and for the rest of the afternoon, Kate explores more of the area, jotting down points of interest, cuisines, and other potential story ideas for *Oliva!* and *New York View.*

That evening she enjoys a quiet dinner on her terrace. As she eats the Caesar salad, made fresh at her tableside, and a Pasta Bolognese with yet another flavorful Italian red sauce, she jots down some ideas for her novel, still a work in progress. Later, sunk beneath the luxurious bedding of her king-size bed and not in the mood to finish the mystery book she had previously started, Kate uses her digital reader's bookstore to pick out a new fiction bestseller whose title—*Living in Bliss*—has caught her eye.

27

Waking up early the following day, Kate grabs a cup of coffee from the hotel's market. Then, she heads out on a four-mile run, after which, upon returning to the hotel famished, she heads straight for the main dining room, where she consumes not the usual Italian breakfast fare— coffee and a pastry or roll—but a traditional "American" breakfast: a Caprese omelet, made just as one would expect with fresh basil, tomato, and buffalo mozzarella, and a toasted rosemary-and-sea salt demi-baguette, fruit cup, and a cappuccino. *Sweet.*

Several hours after breakfast, Kate dips in the resort's impressive infinity pool overlooking the ocean. As she sinks below the pool's surface, allowing herself the day to indulge—minus work—she starts to lose herself, becoming aware only of the sensations of the cool water on her body and the beautiful views surrounding her. Spending relaxing time is healing and food for the soul. Without much to think of besides what she fancies to do and what her next meal will be, in the quiet Kate can examine her life, thoughts, recent happenings, and process—*to let go and let God.*

Kate utters prayers to the Lord, asking for his help to process, find peace, and accept.

When she's not swimming, she reads poolside under the shade of an umbrella. Kate also searches for inspiring words on her Bible app and, with her earbuds on, listens to some of her favorite inspirational pastoral lecturers on YouTube. She finds an overwhelming feeling of well-being in taking these actions and knows it is helping her get to where she needs to go.

Finally, in late afternoon, Kate heads up to her room, where she takes another soak in her suite's jetted tub before she dresses for dinner. Rosa's grandson, Pietro, is scheduled to pick her up at five p.m.

"Buona sereta, cugina," Pietro greets Kate promptly at five o'clock in the resort's lobby, using the word *cugina,* meaning cousin. Looking to be twenty-something, Pietro, with a head of sun-streaked curls and dressed in jeans and a crisp blue T-shirt, is handsome and cheerful. Pietro welcomes Kate with a broad smile and a hug. "No worries, I speak English," he continues with a charming accent.

"Grazie," says Kate as she puts on the helmet Pietro hands her before sliding behind him onto the black Vespa. The gifts she'll be presenting to Rosa for the occasion—a bottle of wine, chocolates, and a box of notecards printed with Kate's Hawaiian photography and Annabella's diary—have been placed in a pretty canvas tote and stored securely under the Vespa's seat. "Ahhh!" Kate screams as Pietro accelerates from zero to maximum speed in seconds.

Pietro chuckles. *"Mi scusi.* Don't be afraid. Put your arms around my waist and hold on. I know these roads like the back of my hand." Pietro offers soothing words to Kate, whose arms have immediately become a vice grip around his waist. "Nonna is so excited to meet you. She's invited the family. We'll be about twenty."

"Twenty?" Kate's voice rises several octaves.

"Yes. Of course. You have to meet *la famiglia.*"

The fact that she'll be meeting all her relatives living in Taormina thrills Kate. As they travel down pretty country roads, Kate becomes more relaxed with Pietro's driving. However, she still holds on to him for dear life. She's glad she decided to wear comfortable white Capri pants with a flattering floral top. Wearing a dress or skirt of any length while traveling on this Vespa might be, for different reasons, dangerous.

The journey to Rosa's has them traveling several miles of winding roads through small gatherings of homes and wide-open spaces. Finally, Pietro turns onto a long dirt road framed with a lava-rock wall and rows of tall palms on either side. The Vespa climbs up and around the path and, at the end of the drive, the beautiful, two-story stone Villa del Mare is revealed. Kate knows the name means "villa of the sea," and the charming, inviting home, with its peachy-pink patina, white wooden shutters, and a wrap-around porch facing the ocean below, certainly lives up to its name. Suddenly, Kate becomes aware of a positive, kinetic energy that permeates the air. The sensation fills her with excitement and anticipation.

This evening is going to be incredible.

Pietro parks his Vespa in the driveway next to others like it. There's also an Alpha Romeo, several Fiats, an SUV, and even a Ferrari.

Rosa, an attractive, seventy-something woman, calls from the balcony, *"Buona Sereta. Hello!"*

"Buona Sereta, Nonna!" Pietro replies as both Kate and Rosa wave their hands wildly.

Rosa suddenly disappears from the terrace, and in the next moment, she's on the multi-colored-limestone-paved driveway, greeting Kate.

"Thank you for the gifts," beams Rosa as Kate hands her the canvas tote filled with goodies.

"Grandma Annabella's diary is also in the tote."

"That will be my reading material before bed this evening. I'm looking forward to it," says Rosa. "Come. Follow me. The family's all here, ready to meet you."

Kate and Pietro follow Rosa up the stairway leading to the terrace landing. Colorful flowers in attractive terracotta pots line the steps, and as Kate ascends, an even more spectacular view of the ocean becomes visible.

To the right of the terrace landing, under the large, roof-covered, tiled patio laden with palms and more colorful flowers showcased in various stone pots, sits a long, rustic, wooden farmhouse-type table surrounded by wicker armchairs padded with fluffy, white linen pillows. Down the center of the table is a beautiful tapestry runner, on top of which are small potted flowers and numerous white candles in glass holders. Adjacent to the table, in a corner with plenty of open space, is a sizeable, carved-wood credenza stacked with dishes, glasses, and other items.

To the left of the landing are a long rattan sofa, coffee table, and a scattering of rattan chairs where many of the family are gathered, sipping their beverages of choice. Relatives pick at an array of antipasto dishes on the coffee table that overflows with selections of olives, cheeses, salami, and prosciutto. There are also roasted red peppers, various grilled vegetables, artichoke hearts, nuts, and slices of bread. Pietro catches Kate's eye as she ogles the feast, and winks.

"We love to *mangiare*." Pietro chuckles and puts his hand to his mouth, pretending to chew.

"Me too," Kate admits with a laugh.

"Welcome, Kate!" declares Rosa, taking Kate's hand and pulling her closer to where everyone is gathered. In the excitement, all Kate can hear is a mishmash of Italian and English greetings and words.

"*Mi scusi, mi scusi*," yells Rosa. "One at a time. And let us all speak English."

Rosa introduces Kate to her husband, Luigi, daughter Greta and Greta's husband, Armando La Rosa (Pietro's parents). Next is Rosa's son, Alberto, his wife, Elisabetta, and their daughter Gina and son Andreas. Also in attendance are Rosa's sister Louisa and her husband, Franco Greco, their son Frederico and his wife, Allegra, and Frederico and Allegra's children, Edoardo, Dario, and Martina. Luigi's brother Alonzo De Luca, his wife, Caterina, and their daughter Chiara, also greet Kate.

"Sit here, Kate," Luigi offers, pulling up a wicker chair to the coffee table. "Pietro, get Kate something to drink."

"Wine? Soda? Iced tea?" Pietro rattles off the choices. "My nonna also made some fresh lemonade with her garden lemons."

"The lemonade sounds lovely. I'll have some of that. Grazie."

"I'm going to check on the sauce," announces Rosa.

"Can I be of any help in the kitchen?" asks Kate.

"No, dear, you stay here. Everything is almost ready."

Dinner is a marvelous array of favorite family courses. The first is a seafood risotto followed by chicken picatta with a side of garlic broccolini and homemade pasta with Rosa's killer red sauce. Next comes a green salad with an array of fresh chopped vegetables and greens from Rosa's garden mixed with balsamic vinegar, olive oil, and seasonings. A cheese and fruit platter follows, and finally, dessert, a decadent tiramisu, along with choices of espresso or cappuccino and Luigi's delicious homemade limoncello.

"I don't think I can move." Kate laughs, rubbing her stomach after dinner. "Everything was so delicious. If you don't mind, Rosa, may I have a copy of your recipes? I love to cook, and I know my husband, Kai, would be thrilled."

"Si, my dear. And when will we meet Kai?"

"He won't arrive for another two weeks. I wish he could have been here for tonight's dinner. He'll be upset he missed it."

"What? No! When he comes to Taormina, we'll have him for dinner." Everyone chimes in about how much they are looking forward to meeting him.

"You mean, do dinner like this again?"

"We dine like this every Sunday night, Kate," says Louisa.

You do?"

"Sunday dinners are a long-standing family tradition," answers Alberto.

"Come to think of it, growing up, my family always dined with my grandparents and aunts, uncles, and cousins," Kate says. "In Kauai, my father lives in our ohana. One of the several meanings of ohana in the Hawaiian language is guesthouse. My husband and I dine with my father and my husband's father, not every Sunday, but most. It's lovely when we do."

"Do you have siblings?" asks Elisabetta.

"Yes. A sister, Carla. She and her husband, Frank, have a son, Lucas. My brother, Derek, is also married with two daughters."

"Do they live near you?" asks Gina, who is close in age to all the other grandchildren at the table.

"No. My sister, brother, and their families live on Long Island, New York." Not knowing how familiar her Italian relatives are with distances in the States, she adds, "That's over five thousand miles from where Kai and I live in Hawaii."

"It must be hard be so far away from them," Greta replies. "I can't imagine living too far from my family."

"We keep in daily touch by text and FaceTime," answers Kate.

Luigi shrugs. "Well, I guess I'm behind the times—old fashioned. I still use only the telephone."

He's adorable, thinks Kate.

"Si, Nonno still uses a dial phone," adds Pietro.

The table breaks out in laughter and Martina leans into her uncle and gives him a big hug and kiss on the cheek. "We love you."

"*Amore Mio.*" Luigi chuckles and, with thumb and forefinger, lovingly wiggles Martina's nose before giving her a peck on the cheek.

The family atmosphere is so friendly and warm that Kate feels as if she's known these people her entire life. For the remainder of the evening, the family recalls funny stories about one another, sharing anecdotes and letting Kate in on several family secrets.

"Thank you so much. It has been a beautiful evening." Kate helps Rosa put away some dishes in the kitchen after most of the family members have departed.

"What are you doing tomorrow?"

"I have a few calls and emails to tend to early morning, but I don't have much planned afterward. Just relaxing."

"If you'd like, I could pick you up, maybe around ten o'clock, and show you around. After that we could spend the day shopping and go to lunch. Then maybe, because you like to cook, we could go to the local market, pick up a few things, and prepare dinner together. You could pack a bag if you'd like to stay overnight."

"Oh, if it's no trouble, I would love that," gushes Kate.

"Buono." Rosa is clearly pleased.

Luigi, wondering what the ladies are discussing as he enters the kitchen, puts his arms around Rosa and kisses the back of her head.

"Kate and I are plotting."

"Oh?"

Rosa laughs. "How to spend your money tomorrow."

"Ah? That so?" Luigi's eyes sparkle, and he starts to tickle Rosa playfully.

"Luigi! Stop!" Rosa lurches away from her husband, who chases her around the kitchen for a second or two.

Then, instead of more tickling, Luigi pulls her close and kisses Rosa's cheek. "That's better, no?"

"Si," chuckles Rosa. "You're so silly sometimes."

"My Kai loves to tickle," chuckles Kate.

"Kate?" asks Pietro, entering the kitchen, ready to take Kate back to the hotel. Kate nods, and after more kisses and hugs, thanks Rosa and Luigi once again for their hospitality.

Back at the hotel later that night, Kate shoots texts to all her family members and Cindy, her sister from another mother. In addition, she includes photos from the evening's dinner. Next, she places a FaceTime call to Olivia, filling her BFF in on all the news.

"What a fabulous time," enthuses Olivia.

"And the flavorful food here—*fantastico!*" yells Kate gleefully, flipping her hands palms up for effect. "Rosa will be taking me to the shops tomorrow. We'll also be going to the local markets to pick up dinner. I'll be cooking with her in her kitchen tomorrow night."

"Wow! You know, that would make a great article. Take lots of notes—and pictures."

"Great idea. I will. I already told Rosa that I wanted tonight's recipes and I took print-worthy photos!"

"That's my Kate." Olivia claps gleefully.

After going over other ideas and getting caught up on the latest in Olivia's life, Kate places a FaceTime call to Kai.

"Hon, you are positively beaming," says Kai after Kate spares no detail of the evening's gathering.

"Get ready to meet them. The family insists."

"Really? They're going to make another family dinner like that again?"

"Apparently, they do it every Sunday night."

"Wow! If the family insists," Kai speaks with an accent that's more New York Italian than native Italian. "I'm in, especially, my stomach."

"How is your tummy-wummy?" Kate pouts, missing her man.

"It's doing okay but missing spooning up to you at night."

"I know. Soon though." Kate sighs. "I love you."

"Love you too, sweetheart. Sleep well tonight, okay? We'll talk again like this tomorrow." Kai blows Kate a few kisses, which she returns before ending the call.

Once in bed Kate finds it hard to turn off her mind, which is constantly replaying the day's events. To help facilitate sleep, she reaches for the novel at her bedside and reads several chapters until she feels her eyes become so heavy that she has no choice but to turn off the night table light and succumb to a night of deep sleep.

28

The following day after the family gathering at Rosa's, Kate wakes early, giving her enough time to exercise in the hotel's gym, shower, dress, and, as Rosa suggested, pack an overnight bag to stay the night at Villa del Mare. After a breakfast of fresh fruit, yogurt, toast, and coffee in the hotel's dining room, Kate returns to her room to check her emails and follow up on correspondence until Rosa calls from the hotel lobby.

"Buongiorno." Kate and Rosa each say as they embrace.

"I see we have similar clothing styles," Rosa adds with a chuckle. Both ladies are casually and chicly dressed in white capris, flowing tops, comfortable walking shoes, and glamorous, wide-brim sun hats.

"Good taste must run in the family," notes Kate.

"Si. *Infatti*, indeed," agrees Rosa.

Kate follows Rosa outside to where Rosa has parked her silver Fiat convertible. Once inside the vehicle, Rosa drives toward town.

"I read part of the diary last night," admits Rosa. "It's incredible to be inside the mind of our grandmother Annabella. My side of the family descends from her daughter, Sienna, and your side from her son, Leonardo."

"That makes Annabella your third and my fourth-great-grandmother," Kate says.

"I think so," Rosa agrees, "but I haven't looked at the entire family tree."

"Neither have I. I'm still researching. I remember my mother talking about Leonardo Ricci, Annabella's son who came to America via Ellis Island in the early nineteen hundreds just after the big earthquake in 1908."

"Oh, yes, that was horrible. Many, many thousands of lives were lost. That earthquake happened early in the morning, and the cities of Messina and Reggio Calabria were almost completely devastated."

"My mother and my grandmother Mary told me that's why Leonardo moved to America. His wife, Anna Maria, was too frightened to stay in Italy. So they moved to Boston and opened a grocery store stocked with cheese, olive oil, wine, and such by our Italian relatives in Italy's import-export business."

"We still get shakers. I'd say one every four or five years, most, thankfully, not the size of the 1908 quake."

"Do they scare you?"

Rosa chuckles. "Not enough for me to leave Taormina. Every place has something. But, for the most part, we are blessed to live here."

"That you are. It is a beautiful, magical place," Kate agrees. "I can't wait to hear what Annabella wrote in her diary," she adds.

"It starts with details about her marriage. She was so happy." Rosa tells Kate what she's read so far and promises to keep her apprised of what else she discovers.

When Rosa and Kate arrive at the Corso Umberto I, the quaint, pedestrian-friendly, traffic-free main boulevard in Taormina, which leads from the Porta Messina to the Porta Catania, the street is full of locals and visitors alike. Named after Umberto I of Savoy, Italy, who reigned from 1878 to 1900, the thoroughfare is home to historic, awe-inspiring architecture—from Arabic to Norman, Gothic, and Baroque—as well as unique, trendy boutiques, popular eateries, and gorgeous views. Much to Kate's delight, Rosa has expertly mapped out a fun-filled day of shopping and lunch.

After several hours of retail therapy, Rosa and Kate select a picturesque café to enjoy a Caprese pizza and salad.

"There's so much you'll have to see while you're in Taormina," enthuses Rosa, sipping her iced tea. "The Ancient Theatre of Taormina, a Greek theatre that dates back to the three hundreds B.C. and was rebuilt by the Romans, the many historic churches, and a tour of the vineyards near Mt. Etna are a must. There's also the gardens of Villa Comunale in Sorrento. And the sailing tour of Taormina Bay is also lovely."

"I plan to make all those stops and more when Kai and my business associate, Olivia Larkin, arrive."

"Ah, yes, Olivia Larkin, the TV talk-show hostess. I started to read *Olivia!* magazine so I could catch up on your articles. You are an excellent writer."

"Grazie," Kate replies, pleased with the compliment.

"So tell me more about your husband Kai, what he does, what your life is like in Kauai."

From their initial talk on the phone to their first in-person meeting yesterday, Rosa feels so familiar to Kate. It's like she's known Rosa all her life. When Kate expresses this sentiment, Rosa admits she feels the same. Kate wonders if it's because Rosa resembles and possesses an attitude similar to her own mother. In fact, Rosa could be her mother's younger sister. The familial and intuitive connection makes Kate comfortable sharing intimate details about her life, such as her recent miscarriage and the appearance of Kai's biological son, Noah.

"My dear, I had two miscarriages." Rosa grabs hold of Kate's free hand. "One before Alberto and one after Greta. I know the pain."

"I'm so sorry." Kate sighs deeply. "Do the pain and sadness ever go away? Do you ever stop wondering what if?"

"Would you like me to be honest?"

Kate grimaces as if she knows what Rosa will say.

"No, my dear, they do not." Rosa shakes her head. "But like all loss, it becomes a little less, and it is important to go through the stages of grief."

"Yes, denial, isolation, anger, bargaining, depression, and acceptance, then repeat."

"Correct. You've seen a therapist to help you with your feelings?"

"Yes. I felt I was making some headway and then BAM. Noah enters stage right."

"And how did that make you feel?"

"I guess I became extremely aware of what Kai and I lost—*our* baby. And here's this stranger claiming paternity."

"Noah is Kai's for sure?"

"The DNA test confirmed it."

"And this bothers you because?"

Kate thinks in prolonged silence. Then the tears begin to fall and she quickly wipes away the wetness from her cheeks. "I guess because I wanted our first child . . . *any* child in our lives . . . to be born out of our love."

"Do you think having Noah appear will make Kai love you any less?"

"No."

"Love any children you both may bring into this world any less?"

"No."

"Do you think knowing Noah is Kai's biological child will strain your marriage?"

"I think it already has. But the problem is me. Kai has been so loving and understanding. I'm sure his head is reeling. I know it is. But I also know what an emotional basket case I've been, crying at the drop of a hat, avoiding discussions about Noah with Kai, and sometimes ignoring that it's happening. I'm ashamed to say, I've also been short tempered with my husband on occasion and avoidant. It's like I can't control myself regarding this topic."

"My dear, I think it is good that you came for some relaxing time in Taormina. You need some quiet time to process and reflect. Since you are a writer, write about it. Keep a diary—*like Annabella.* Sometimes writing down our feelings helps us process and come to terms with what we need to face."

"That's an excellent idea. I'll start. Grazie," says Kate.

"And if I may be so bold as to say—"

"Yes?"

"I believe you need to forgive yourself . . . and then, perhaps, Kai."

"Forgive myself?" Kate hadn't thought of that.

"Forgiveness is extending mercy to yourself and others who have harmed us, even if not intentional. You might start by forgiving yourself or your body for this miscarriage. Express your feelings about your pain, lost hopes, and dreams. Concerning Noah and Kai, extend empathy, compassion, and respect by looking at things from their point of view, their history, and their pain. Doing so will help with your understanding and healing. Learning to forgive also comes from being of service, recognizing and appreciating the beauty in the world, and sharing love and friendship. We will always hold a special place in our hearts and continue to grieve, but when we focus on our blessings, the positive, being of service, it is healing to our hearts, mind, and soul. There's a Bible saying I've always loved—Proverbs Seventeen, Verse Nine: *'Love prospers when a fault is forgiven, but dwelling on it separates close friends.'* You are such a treasure, Kate, a loving, warm woman, and you have so much to live for and to give. Pray and ask the

Lord for assistance, guidance, and peace. Prayer is powerful, and He wants to hear from us and help us. I hope I don't offend, but I say all this to you because *I* also need to remember."

"I talk to God daily. I truly appreciate this conversation, Rosa. It's touched me deeply, and I'll start to focus on the things you've shared."

"Well, I believe there's nothing as marvelous as appreciating the here and now with a cappuccino paired with freshly made cannoli. There's a shop close by—Roberto's—the best in town. Can I tempt you?

Kate laughs. "You had me at *cannoli.*"

After indulging in a creamy, sweet ricotta cannolo dipped in praline almonds and powdered sugar at Roberto's, Rosa and Kate continue their shopping tour. Kate's purchases include several lovely, original, hand-painted floral scarves for Olivia, her other Nā Pīkake sisters, her sister, Carla, BFF Cindy, and herself. In one of the local shops featuring a variety of leather goods—including purses, briefcases, luggage, belts, and other items—Kate scores an attractive Italian leather wallet for Kai and, for herself, a diary. For the diary's jacket, Kate selects a gorgeous, hand-crafted, refillable leather cover embossed with a stunning design of sunflowers. The coat, adorned with a leather front clasp and vintage snaps, fits perfectly over the hard-backed diary.

"If we head to the square market right now to pick up some things for dinner, we'll make it in time before it closes," says Rosa, looking at her watch.

The market is a gorgeous mix of vibrant colors, exciting sounds, and a montage of faces, young and old. Kate marvels at the fantastic displays of green lettuces, zucchini, cucumbers, artichokes, and groupings of scallions and asparagus tied with string. There are also deep-purple eggplants, fire-engine-red peppers and tomatoes in various shapes and sizes, luscious yellow lemons, succulent strawberries, and peaches with shining red-orange skins, beautiful plump green and red grapes, and other produce delights showcased in crates, baskets, and boxes. In between helping Rosa with dinner selections, Kate can't resist whipping out her phone to take some photos she knows she'll post on her gardenofaloha.com site and for use in her magazine articles.

"Do you like stuffed artichokes?" asks Rosa as she picks through the crate of round-stemmed olive-green buds made of large, overlapping petals.

"Do I? I adore them! My grandma Mary made them all the time.

"Stuffed with herbed breadcrumbs and Parmesan cheese?"

"YES!"

"Buono." Rosa adds several artichokes into her canvas shopping bag filled with leafy salad greens, arugula, fresh basil, eggplant, olives, mushrooms, tomatoes, and a wedge of sharp Parmigiano Reggiano cheese. Kate adds in a few plump lemons for the lemony pasta they'll make for the *primi*, the meal's first course.

"Now the swordfish," says Rosa.

Kate follows Rosa to where Giuseppe, a plump, balding, sixty-something man wearing a full-length chef's apron, yells answers to the questions posed by shoppers.

"Buongiorno, Rosa!" calls Giuseppe, smiling. Rosa introduces Kate, and then Rosa and Giuseppe converse in Italian.

"Giuseppe always flirts with me," Rosa says with a chuckle after she orders the fish they'll grill for dinner. "He's always giving me specials other customers aren't privy to—or so he says."

The ladies laugh as Giuseppe hands Rosa the large swordfish steak wrapped in paper and plastic. He winks at her, smiling devilishly.

"Grazie." Rosa pays Giuseppe the exact amount in cash.

Giuseppe blows kisses to Rosa and Kate. *"Bella donne."*

"He is quite flirtatious," says Kate, nudging Rosa playfully.

"Ah, he's harmless." Rosa laughs. "Besides, I know his wife, Sophia. She's a no-nonsense woman who keeps him in line."

29

A large, wooden center island with a white quartz countertop sits at the center of Rosa's bright, modern kitchen featuring elegant and timeless antique white cabinets, Old World-style stone walls, honey-colored, rustic beamed ceiling, and state-of-the-art stainless-steel appliances. The sliders to the patio are open, allowing a cool, welcoming breeze to flow through the room.

Kate stands at the center island, serving as Rosa's sous chef.

"We'll have lemon pasta for the primi course," announces Rosa as she instructs Kate to grate the zest of several lemons into a blue-and-white striped ceramic bowl, using a long, thin, stainless-steel cheese grater.

While Kate grates, Rosa readies the tomato, basil, black olive, and caper relish for the swordfish her husband, Luigi, will grill.

"What can I do next?" asks Kate.

"Let's put the vegetables on the skewers. Luigi will grill them with the fish."

Kate stacks each skewer with slices of onion, tomato, eggplant, and mushroom and dusts them with some extra virgin olive oil and herbs.

"Have you ever had pizzelle?" asks Rosa about the well-loved, round waffle cookie made with anise.

"Oh, yes, I love them! My gram Mary used to make them at the holidays. The anise tastes just like black licorice."

"I like to serve them with gelato, like an ice cream sandwich. I made some last week. We'll have them for dessert tonight." Rosa winks. "*Delizioso.*"

Later that evening, after the delicious meal and more conversation, Rosa and Luigi retire to their bedroom, where Rosa spends half the night reading more of Annabella's diary.

Following Rosa's suggestion earlier that day, Kate begins

writing in her new diary in the beautifully appointed guest chambers down the hall. A king-size bed with a stunning white-tufted headboard and a sumptuous mattress, equal to anything one would find in any five-star hotel, sits in front of a classic antique-white armoire housing a large screen TV behind its doors. The cozy room also boasts a wood-beamed ceiling, stone fireplace, and a luxurious en suite bathroom with a sunken tub. Kate sits at an antique desk with a window view, pen in hand. Although it is night, and tiny dots of residential light illuminate the hillside, the expansive dark sky over the ocean is filled with sparkling diamonds. Every so often Kate lifts her eyes from the page to look out at the dark horizon as if in a trance while she delves deeply into her feelings.

Dear Diary,

At this moment I am sitting at the most exquisite, antique, inlaid-wood desk overlooking a picture-perfect view. Stars hang low above the ocean, blanketing the night sky. A cool breeze blows through my cozy guest chambers, which are decorated in soothing pastels with a honey-wood-beamed ceiling and luxurious furnishings. Rosa told me tonight that our family has lived in this villa overlooking the Ionian Sea for generations.

I feel so blessed to have met Rosa and Luigi, as well as the rest of my newly found relatives in Taormina. Tonight, Rosa is reading more in my fourth-great-grandmother (and her third-great-grandmother) Annabella's diary. As the journal is written in Italian, Rosa will share the contents with me.

It's incredible that, had I not investigated my mother's family tree through the Generations site, I would have never met these family members. I've only been here a few days, yet I feel a deep connection to them. Rosa's welcoming demeanor and gentle temperament remind me of my dear mother. Insightful, warm, and caring, I felt an immediate bond between Rosa and me. She expressed feeling the same toward me.

I like that, in Italy, I see the bonds of Lu Famiglia everywhere. Family is everything. Young and old gather in the squares, affectionate and demonstrative. While I'm sure there are many kinds of people and situations, both positive and negative, I can attest that I feel the power of the family.

I have also been brought up, thankfully, to appreciate familial bonds. Perhaps that's why I'm still trying to make sense of and process the loss of our little one. I was devastated, and I know Kai was too. However, he held it together to be strong for me as best he could.

One night, at home in Kauai, when I got up to get a glass of water from the kitchen, I could hear Kai's sobs through the open screen door. I was transfixed. It felt surreal. I waited until his cries subsided before I joined him on the patio. When he saw me, he quickly wiped the wetness from his cheeks. I know he didn't want to upset me. I sat beside him on the lanai sofa, taking his hand and laying my head against his shoulder. He put his arms around me, and we sat there in silence, holding one another for I don't know how long.

I miss Kai, and I wish he were here with me. I'm comforted he will be soon. However, I'm also glad I've had some time on my own in Italy, as I know it's been good for me to process and work to come to terms with all that has transpired.

I feel ashamed that I've been short-tempered and emotional with Kai. Yet, when my thoughts turn to the reality of Noah's existence, Kai's biological son through sperm donation, and whom Kai never intended to meet, I feel paralyzed. Upset. Angry. Not myself. I'm not sure what this fact—or his existence—means for our life moving forward. If I am honest with myself, I know I'm also angry and emotional that I miscarried, that I was not able to give Kai a child at this time, and then Noah appears. So often during the day— and at night—I think about our child and what might have been. What he might have been and achieved. I wanted him to be, not Noah. There, I said it. I know this must be your will, God, but I have difficulty accepting it. Please help me, Lord. Please grant me the serenity to accept the things I cannot change, the courage to change the things I can, and the wisdom to know the difference.

Kate

After Kate writes the well-known Serenity Prayer in her diary, she finds she has nothing more to divulge. So she places the journal in her suitcase for safekeeping, after which she washes and readies for bed. Finally, she falls into a deep sleep with a full day of activities and emotions behind her.

In her dream, Kate walks the sandy shoreline at her favorite Anini Beach on Kauai's North Shore. She is the only soul for miles on the peaceful coast, and the colors of the ocean turn from clear to shades of aqua and blue at the center of the sea as she looks out onto the horizon. Then, suddenly, Kate feels a presence next to her. It's her late mother, Catherine. Acknowledging one another with love in their eyes and a knowing smile, the two women walk in silence, arm in arm.

In the distance, Kate sees two figures walking toward her and her mother. As they move closer, Kate can see they are males, similar in height.

In the next instant, they are directly in front of her—Kai and Noah.

Waking abruptly, Kate surveys her surroundings. At first, she's a little confused but then remembers she's at Rosa and Luigi's. Then, a little startled by the dream, which felt like it was happening in real time, Kate rises out of bed. A silver tray housing an insulated steel ice bucket and glass water pitcher filled with water flavored with lemon slices sits on the nearby dresser. Kate uncovers the bucket with one hand, picks up silver tongs with the other, and places ice cubes in a glass tumbler. Then, pouring lemon water to the brim of the glass, she drinks and paces the room, pondering her vibrant dream.

Mom felt like she was standing beside me. I could feel her arm in mine. Then Kai and Noah appeared. What did this dream mean? Was it just a result of what I thought about when I wrote in my diary before bed?

Kate can feel her body and eyelids becoming heavy once again. Sleep is seconds away as she sinks into the luxurious bedding beneath the cool, silky sheets.

30

Taormina, Province of Messina, Italy, 1874

Annabella's Diary, 1874:

My dear husband Stefano's cough seems to be getting worse. He's so pale and has lost quite a bit of weight. Sometimes at night he even suffers night sweats, and our maid Flora has to change the soaked bedsheets. I am so worried about him.

At first Stefano had a simple cough. We thought it was nothing. In the past he worked all hours helping to build our family's import-export business. Now he barely has enough energy to get out of bed. Although he wishes to return to the work he loves, our parents insist that he care for his health and get well. Under the doctor's orders, Stefano is to rest, eat a balanced, healthy diet, and spend time every day outdoors in the fresh air.

I am happy that he hasn't lost his sense of humor or positive spirit. I think this will bode well in his recovery.

Every afternoon, fulfilling the doctor's wishes for Stefano to receive a daily dose of sunshine and fresh air, we play cards at our favorite spot in the garden. These moments are gold to me. We talk about the local news—Stefano reads the paper in bed every morning with his breakfast—we discuss happenings with our family and friends. We receive gifts almost daily—flowers, fruit baskets, loving cards—and well wishes for Stefano's return to optimum health.

Sometimes, however, playing cards and conversation is taxing on Stefano, so much so that he has taken to napping on the garden lounge chair, and during this time, I paint while he sleeps. Today, my subject was my love. The golden light that sifted through the palms and scarlet bougainvillea against the beautiful turquoise sea surrounding Stefano was stunning. He was so peaceful, sprawled out on the lounge, his straw hat partially covering his face. It was the perfect image and compelled me to paint while he slept. I have the essential elements completed, so he will not have to sit for me tomorrow when I add the finishing touches.

As I write in this diary tonight, I watch my dear Stefano's labored breathing as he sleeps. It pains me and worries me so much.

Dear loving Father in heaven, I know you are with us and that you know my heart. Therefore, I humble myself to you and implore you to please restore my beloved Stefano's health. He loves you so, and he has so much life to live and love to give here on earth.

Annabella

Taormina, Province of Messina, Italy, Present Day

Rosa wipes a tear as she translates Annabella's diary entry to Kate after breakfast the following day.

"Does he return to health?" asks Kate.

"I'll read more tonight and let you know. According to Annabella's diary, Stefano has suffered like this for some time. By the time she writes this entry, he appears to be getting worse."

"Heartbreaking. I suppose I could do more research on the Generations site, but I like hearing the news direct from Annabella's diary."

"Come, I want to show you something."

Kate follows Rosa into the library. Beautiful floor-to-ceiling wooden bookshelves adorned with ornate carvings and filled with books, art, family photos, and artifacts cover three walls of the study. A sizeable inlaid wooden desk sits in the center of the room and faces French doors in the fourth wall that lead to a terrace with an ocean view. Two paintings in vintage, gold-leaf frames hang on each side of the double doors. One of the paintings is just as Annabella described in her diary.

"It's the painting of Stefano sleeping!" yelps Kate. She runs to examine the beautiful oil. "Wow. It's gorgeous!" Kate takes in the details of the artistry, noting Annabella's barely visible name in the bottom right-hand corner. When she looks to the other side of the door, Annabella's signature also appears on a stunning oil of the Taormina coast, complete with a view of a snowcapped Mt. Etna. "Are there more of Annabella's paintings?"

Rosa smiles and waves for Kate to follow her. She shows Kate other works displayed in the hallways and rooms.

"How did you come by them?"

"My parents and grandparents told me that Annabella and her husband lived here. Then, years ago, a chest with some of her belongings was found containing a number of her paintings. When Luigi and I remodeled the villa some time back, we wanted to keep the charm and add a bit of family history, so we hung a few of her paintings."

"You did a marvelous job," acknowledges Kate. "I love the feel of the place."

Rosa nods. "Grazie. Would you like to take one of Annabella's paintings home? You could choose one, and I could have it shipped."

"I would love that!" enthuses Kate, her voice rising several octaves.

"Let's take a look." Rosa shows Kate into a large storage room where a few other paintings—both watercolors and oils—are displayed on the walls. An oil of a colorful terrace garden overlooking the ocean and coastline holds Kate's interest. There's also another spectacular work of Taormina's ancient Greek-Roman theatre that Kate visited with Rosa.

"I can't seem to decide. All the paintings are amazing."

"You can have both."

"Really?"

"Of course. We have a lot of Annabella's art. You're family. You should have a piece of our family history and treasures."

"Grazie. Ti amo." Kate throws her arms around Rosie in a giant bear hug.

"Ti amo, Bella."

After enjoying a second morning cappuccino, Rosa invites Kate to stay another night. The two ladies decide to take another trip into town, this time to the flower mart and to have lunch by the shore. Upon returning to the villa in mid-afternoon, Rosa promises to show Kate how she makes homemade pasta, which they'll enjoy for dinner that evening.

"This is so much fun, sharing the day with you," gushes Rosa as they drive the windy road into town. "By the way, my daughter,

Greta, and her husband, Armondo, will join us for dinner tonight."

"Will your son, Alberto, and his wife be coming?"

"Alberto and Chaira have a previous engagement, but they'll be able to have dessert with us."

Kate loves the idea of family dinners. Growing up, she and her sister, Carla, were always mother's helpers in the kitchen, not only for family dinners but for entertaining friends, which was almost a weekly occurrence, with Sundays after church spent sharing a meal with both maternal and paternal grandparents. Perhaps that's why, to this day, she loves to cook and entertain.

"Rosa, would you mind if I take videos and still photos of you making pasta? I have a blog that I'd like to share them on."

"You didn't tell me I'd need hair and makeup today," Rosa protests, laughing.

With her classic lines, beautiful features, and hair pulled back in an elegant chignon, Rosa is effortlessly gorgeous, thinks Kate.

"Of course, I would be honored to be featured. What's your blog's focus?"

"Sometimes, I write posts that are a continuation of the subjects I interview in my magazine articles. For example, I have a section where I post my photography and another where I post my recipe creations."

Since childhood, Kate has always enjoyed creating recipes using healthy ingredients and adding different herbs and spices for various tastes. She has kept a file of her recipes for years and now has an extensive collection.

"I know you write novels, but do you ever think about compiling all your recipes into a cookbook?" asks Rosa.

"Maybe. Someday. It's been a dream of mine to do that. I certainly have enough material."

"That's what life is all about. Living our dreams. And there's no time like the present to start." Rosa turns briefly to wink at Kate.

Kate and Rosa decide to have lunch at a pretty seaside café where they dine on grilled salmon with a tangy citrus-mustard sauce presented over a bed of thin julienne strips of zucchini, carrots, and peppers.

"I started writing in my diary last night," shares Kate as she sips an iced tea before taking another bite of the succulent salmon. "It was amazing what came out. And my dream was—"

"Dream?"

"I had the most realistic dream. In it I was walking on Anini Beach, one of my favorite beaches on Kauai's North Shore. Then my mom appeared by my side, and we walked arm and arm for a while. It felt so real, so comforting. Even though we didn't speak a word, I felt the love and connection. A short time later, I saw two men walking in the distance, and suddenly they were right in front of me. It was Kai and Noah. I woke instantly."

"How did the dream make you feel?"

"I felt good in the dream. Walking with my mom was wonderful and soothing. When Kai and Noah appeared, I was surprised and a bit shocked, but it wasn't a bad thing. Seeing their faces close in front of me woke me, though."

"Maybe you had the dream because you started to examine your feelings and began writing in your diary."

"I think so," says Kate in agreement.

The ladies eat until Kate asks, "Rosa, see the picture on the wall beside us of the young girl with the halo holding the white lily flowers? Do you know who she is?"

"She is Saint Maria Goretti. Her story is a sad one, but one of ultimate forgiveness."

"What happened to her?"

"Maria was an eleven-year-old Italian girl who was stabbed to death in 1902 while resisting a sexual assault from her known assailant."

"How horrible."

"She warded off her attacker, preventing the rape, claiming she would rather die than submit. However, before Maria succumbed to her injuries, she forgave her killer. Years later, her murderer, still unrepentant for his crime, had a dream where Maria, in a garden, handed him white lilies—supposedly there were fourteen—which burned his hands. The vision inspired the killer's repentance and conversion to the faith. He later became a lay brother at a monastery. Maria was canonized in 1950, becoming the patron saint of purity, young women, and victims of assault. But the most important takeaway of her story is not the murder, it's how Maria forgave her enemy, even beyond the grave, and the miracle her faith, mercy, and forgiveness made in her killer's life."

"I didn't know about St. Maria. But as a journalist I want to learn more."

Later that evening, in the guest bedroom at Villa del Mare, and after her FaceTime calls with Kai and other friends and family, Kate emails Olivia a list of story ideas she has been researching since arriving in Taormina. Then she investigates more about the life of St. Maria Goretti and learns that Maria was born to a farming family. Her father died of malaria when Maria was nine, after which her family shared a home with another family, the Serenellis. Maria helped her family by cooking, sewing, housekeeping, and watching her youngest sibling, Teresa, while her mother, brothers, and sisters worked in the fields. Maria's family was devoted to each other and the Lord.

However, when Maria was eleven, she was fatally attacked by the Serenellis' eighteen-year-old son, Alessandro. According to Kate's research, Maria warded off Alessandro's advances and attempts numerous times, exclaiming, "It is a sin! God does not want it!" Upon hearing Maria's words, Alessandro fatally stabbed her, but before she died, she said, "I forgive you."

Alessandro was eventually released from prison many years after the crime. He begged Maria's mother for forgiveness, which she gave, saying, "If my daughter can forgive him, who am I to withhold forgiveness?"

Moved by St. Maria's story, Kate wipes a few tears from her cheeks. She thinks about the incredible mercy Maria and her mother showed Alessandro, who eventually was repentant and transformed.

The power of faith, mercy, and forgiveness, thinks Kate. As she slips between the bedsheets her last thoughts are of St. Maria, and, praying for her loved ones, Kate asks the Lord for protection, insight, and guidance.

31

Taormina, Province of Messina, Italy, 1874

Annabella's Diary, 1874:

> *I pour my heart out to you. Yesterday was the saddest day of my life. So heartbreaking that I could not even write to you.*
>
> *My beloved Stefano died just after dawn. He is with our Heavenly Father now in paradise. But, oh, I am broken. I feel physical pain in my heart so searing I can barely walk, and my eyes are red from crying. My dearest has left his physical form. Why this early fate for such a wonderful, loving husband and son? His poor mother and father are also inconsolable, and my parents are devastated and worried for me.*
>
> *I'm not sure why the Lord needed my Stefano, but I pray for understanding and to keep strong, to have the faith to live the life I have left. I wonder how I will endure. Everything feels surreal to me. I cannot sleep nor eat. My thoughts are only on my love, what we had, what we hoped to have, and what we will not have. Oh, the pain. Help me, Lord. Please hold me up.*
>
> *I cannot explain it, but when I feel I will lose my mind or I cannot breathe, I feel a presence. Is it Stefano? The Lord? My guardian angel? Whoever you are, please stay with me and see me through this devastation, for I cannot conceive of any light in my future.*
>
> *Annabella*

Taormina, Province of Messina, Italy, Present Day

"Buongiorno, Bella." Rosa greets Kate good morning with a kiss on both cheeks. Kate can smell the delicious aroma of the coffee beans brewing.

"Cappuccino?"

Rosa laughs. "Is the Pope Catholic? I made a nice American breakfast—spinach and mushroom frittata with goat cheese, fresh herbs, and some baguette toasted with avocado."

"Rosa, you're spoiling me, you know." Kate comes up behind Rosa at the stove and squeezes her tightly.

"Buongiorno, Katie!" cries Luigi dramatically as he enters the kitchen and embraces Kate. He plants a wet kiss on his wife's lips and another on her cheek. "Smells delicious, amore mio,"

"Luigi, make a round of cappuccinos for us," Rosa says. "You always make them so delicious."

"Ah, I see what you do." Luigi chuckles and winks at Rosa, then says to Kate, "Flattery, a way to a man's heart."

"Oh, I thought it was through good food," teases Kate with a chuckle.

"Ha! Good one," Luigi admits.

"Come on now—the cappuccinos," instructs Rosa.

"She's the kitchen boss," Luigi whispers to Kate.

"I heard that, amore mio, and yes, that is correct," Rosa says playfully.

After a lovely breakfast on the terrace overlooking the gardens and sea, Luigi heads off to a work meeting, leaving Rosa and Kate to spend the rest of the morning leisurely enjoying another cappuccino and more conversation. Kate is transfixed as Rosa translates more of Annabella's diary.

"Anabella and Stefano were only married six years. How sad," comments Kate. "Consumption was a terrible thing. So many died, young and old alike. I remember reading it was rampant from the sixteen hundreds to the nineteen hundreds, and even in ancient times. Thank goodness a cure was discovered in the nineteen forties, I believe. It's amazing how it affected some people and not others." She pauses to take a sip of her cappuccino, then continues. "Do you know if Annabella got sick?"

"So far, no. But Annabella is beside herself with grief. It's painful to read."

"She does marry later," comments Kate. "Otherwise, we wouldn't be sitting here drinking our cappuccinos. I'll be anxious to find out more from her diary."

After breakfast, Kate, at her desk in the guest room, logs on to the Generations site. She has received more clues about her mother's family tree. From what Kate learns, it appears Annabella married again—a year later.

Wow. The next year. Did Anabella marry just to marry, her heart still broken?

"Grazie once more, for such a lovely time last night, Rosa." Kate embraces Rosa on the steps of her hotel the following day.

"The pleasure was ours. The family is looking forward to meeting Kai. Tell Olivia she is welcome, too. When does she arrive?"

"Tomorrow afternoon. We have some work to do when she gets here. Then Kai will be here the following week. I think they'll both want to take you up on that offer."

"*È perfetto*. Perfect. Let me know what works best. In the meantime, I'll keep you apprised of anything more I learn from Annabella's diary."

Rosa and Kate embrace one more time before Kate makes her way into her hotel.

Kate spends the remainder of the day in front of her computer on her hotel balcony, answering emails, researching additional points of interest for story ops for *Olivia!* and *New York View* magazines, and following up on ancestry clues on the Generations website before writing in her diary, now a new daily ritual.

Dear Diary,

Rosa is updating me on what she finds reading Annabella's diary.

I think about Annabella and her pain after her beloved Stefano died, yet she had the strength to go on, marry again, and have children. And what courage my relatives Leonardo and Anna Maria had to travel by boat across the sea, moving to a new country with new customs and a different language after the loss of relatives during the devastating 1908 earthquake in Messina. I am awed by the courage, strength, and fortitude of these amazing souls! They fill my thoughts tonight as I sit comfortably on my terrace overlooking the beauty of the calm Ionian Sea as the sun slowly sets beyond the horizon and the sky turns into a kaleidoscopic masterpiece.

Kate

32

The following afternoon, Olivia texts Kate about each leg of her journey to Italy—traveling from Kauai to Manhattan, the evening layover spent in luxury at The Huntington, a chic five-star hotel overlooking Central Park, boarding the plane at JFK, landing in Rome, and, finally, traveling via private car to Villa Bella Vista.

"Hey, girlfriend!" shouts Olivia joyfully as Kate opens their suite's door.

"OMG! I'm so glad you're here. It's wonderful to see a familiar face from home." Kate sits on the king-size bed in Olivia's room while Olivia excitedly relays the details of her travels and the latest work news.

"*Olivia!*'s TV producer—"

"—Morgan Armstrong?" interjects Kate.

"Yes. Morgan set up some fantastic arrangements for us based on the suggestions you've emailed me. To start, a private tour of Mt. Etna followed by lunch and wine tasting at an Etna winery. They'll also be a cooking class with one of the area's top chefs at his hillside home, a sunset-sail dinner cruise on the bay, etcetera. She's also coordinated a local videographer and photographer we've worked with before to film us. So we'll be able to use the pieces on the TV show, in the online magazine, social media, and the print publication."

"Wow! That came together fast. I guess that's why Morgan gets paid the big bucks."

"You got that right!" Olivia nods, energized by the thought of the stories to be covered.

"I'm not sure if I have the right wardrobe to be filmed and photographed," frets Kate.

"No worries. Hair, makeup, and wardrobe have been arranged for the filming days."

Kate chuckles. "Can I get Morgan to work for me too?"

"Ha!" laughs Olivia. "Say, I'm starving. All this excitement, and my body clock's slightly off. Is there somewhere we can grab a bite close to home?"

"The villa's dining room is *magnifico*—elegant—yet you can dress casually and dine serenely, looking at incredible ocean views and eating fabulous fresh food."

"Sold."

As Olivia and Kate dine on freshly made bruschetta on garlic toast and seafood linguine in a savory lemon-garlic-butter sauce, Kate shares her emotional experience of meeting new relatives, and Olivia fills her in on all the local Hanalei news. "Oh! I can't believe I almost forgot to mention it. Alia's getting married!" exclaims Olivia.

Olivia excitedly relates the details of her daughter's engagement. Alia's loving husband-to-be—Robert, like Alia, is an ER doctor in the Boston-based hospital where they both work.

Kate's mind wanders back to shortly after her marriage to Kai, when she first learned about Olivia's daughter. At the time, one night when Kai was working late, Kate barely escaped a home intrusion assault at the Weke cottage. However, her quick thinking led her to outsmart her attacker and escape with only a few scratches. Unfortunately, the incident resulted in some out-of-character behavior from Olivia.

Nevertheless, Kate's intuition convinced her that something was up with her friend. With a gentle hand, Kate navigated the troubled waters and helped Olivia share her decades-held secret—that she had been raped as a young teenager, and had a daughter, which she put up for adoption.

Olivia eventually found the strength to meet and forge a friendship with Alia, who by that time was a grown woman. Kate is proud of her friend's bravery and knows that she can learn a lesson or two from Olivia about acceptance.

"That's fantastic news, and Robert sounds perfect for Alia," Kate says. "Have they set a date yet?"

"Not yet, but they're looking into venues for next summer."

"How's Alia's mom and dad?"

"Doing well."

Kate remembers that it was difficult for Alia's mom when she learned Olivia was the birth mother. She fretted over her daughter being at the center of media attention. However, with Alia's and her family's permission, Olivia enlisted Kate to share their story—breaking the news first in *Olivia!* magazine before any other outlet could run with the story. Although the in-depth article initially met with hoopla due to

Olivia's iconic status, the frenzy quickly dissipated because everyone involved handled the story with dignity and transparency. Olivia's grace and courage increased her image on the stage of public opinion.

Pulling herself back to the present, Kate relays the story of St. Maria Goretti to Olivia and fills Olivia in on the fact that she's working on extending mercy and forgiveness.

"But you have nothing to forgive," states Olivia.

"Oh, but I do. I need to forgive my body for the miscarriage, forgive Kai for his involvement with the existence of Noah, forgive Noah for just being Noah."

"Are you there yet?"

"Not quite. I'm still trying to find peace in my mind and soul. Learning about St. Maria, talking to Rosa, who suffered two miscarriages herself, learning how my ancestors overcame odds with faith and fortitude, and conversing with you about your courage and faith has been extremely helpful. Have you forgiven your attacker and all that transpired?"

"It took me many years, as you know. However, after connecting with Alia, meeting her parents, and seeing what an amazing job they did with her, I can honestly say I forgive my situation and circumstance and forgive myself for putting her up for adoption. And, yes, I can extend some mercy to my unknown attacker. However, to be honest, I'm still working on that. I am extraordinarily thankful for all the love my grandparents gave me during that time and throughout my life while they were still with us. My parents died young, as you know, and my grandparents *were* my parents. I'm also thankful for Grant, Kai, and all my friends and associates. If it weren't for all of you, I wouldn't be where I am today—in my heart and soul or in my career."

"And I am eternally grateful to you, my dear friend, for your caring, love, guidance, introduction to Kauai and Kai, for our work together," returns Kate. "We are blessed."

"Yes, we are. Let's thank the good Lord for that." Olivia lifts her glass in a toast, and Kate does the same.

In her dream Kate strolls the dirt and stone path of the stunning Weke cottage garden. The exquisite landscape, lovingly planted by her and Kai, overflows with scarlet, pink, and white hibiscus. There are swaying palms in all shapes and sizes, birds of paradise, and ruby and yellow heliconia among other flowering delights. Kate's senses are heightened as she delights in the sounds of nature—the 'Apapane, I'iwi, Kaua'i Elepaio, and other birdsongs, intermixed with a chorus of crickets, and the music the wind makes rustling through the leaves. Then Kai appears and places his large, manly hand over Kate's petite one. This simple, comforting gesture makes Kate feel warm and protected. The two lovers walk in harmony. Then Kate stops, curious. Behind a monstera plant's large perforated green leaves, she glimpses bits of white. To her surprise, when she pushes back the bush, a bed of gorgeous white lilies basking in a golden glow is revealed.

Kate wakes from the vibrant dream, but images of the pulsating, life-like lilies remain in her mind. Wide awake, she picks up her phone on the nightstand and googles images and paintings of St. Maria Goretti.

Those lilies St. Maria holds are just like the ones in my dream.

33

———

"Buongiorno!" Fabio, a friendly, attractive man in his mid-forties, enthusiastically greets Kate and Olivia the following morning. Fabio is their private guide and driver for the day tour of the Etna countryside. Olivia and Kate, dressed comfortably in their yoga pants, flowy tops, sneakers, and SPF wide-brimmed sunhats, follow Fabio down to the resort lobby where they are met by a videographer/photographer, Enzo Abate, hired by Olivia's TV producer. After hellos are exchanges, the group piles into a luxurious, air-conditioned Mercedes minivan.

"*Pronto ad andare?* Oops, *mi scusi,*" apologies Fabio with a chuckle. "Ready to go?" Fabio's Italian accent and gestures are quite endearing and are what one would expect for a native Italian speaking English.

"He's adorable," whispers Olivia to Kate, who nods in agreement.

"What's on today's agenda, Fabio?" asks Kate.

"First, we travel through some pretty towns and farmlands to Etna, where we will walk along the volcanic terrain, see the craters, and take photos. Then afterward, a private farm-to-table dining experience at a farmhouse in Alcantara. You will like!"

"Oh, I'm sure we will," answers Olivia.

"Especially the farm-to-table food and wine and dining experience. Organic produce grown in fertile, volcanic soil tastes amazing!" adds Kate.

"You have delicious-tasting produce in Hawaii, no?"

"Yes, we do. We also have rich, volcanic soil and are very thankful."

"Mt. Etna is one of the tallest, most active volcanos in Europe," mentions Fabio. "It covers about 1,190 kilometers—459 square miles, with a basal circumference of 140 kilometers or 87 miles. It is about two-and-a-half-times larger than Mount Vesuvius, the next largest of Italy's active volcanos."

"How many active volcanos does Italy have?" asks Olivia.

"Three. Vesuvius near Naples, Mt. Etna in Sicily, and Mt.

Stromboli, on the island of Stromboli on the north coast of Sicily."

Fabio continues to answer Kate's and Olivia's questions as they travel through quaint towns and lush farmlands. Like Hawaii, there are lava-rock walls and even houses and churches made of lava rock. They drive through the picturesque Sicilian countryside, home to lemon, orange, and olive groves. As they get closer to Mt. Etna, the terrain starts to change—the soil and earth blackened and treeless from the volcanic ash, with only patches of green dotting the surrounding hills. At Enzo's and Kate's request, Fabio parks the van at various points so photos and video can be taken.

When the group finally arrives at their destination, about 2,000 meters—or a mile and a quarter—up the mountain, patches of green can no longer be viewed, only dark earth as far as the eye can see. Fabio shows them around ancient craters, recent lava flow areas still smoking, and other-world-looking terrain.

"Okay, I think I've seen enough earth today. I'm famished!" exclaims Olivia several hours later. She pulls out a bag of mixed nuts from her fanny pack. "How about you, Kate?" Olivia takes a handful of nuts and then hands the bag to Kate.

"Yup. Ready for the food and wine," Kate says with a chuckle as she pours out a palmful of nuts in her hand before handing the pouch back to Olivia.

"Grazie," says Fabio when Olivia promptly hands him the bag. Then he distributes bottled water to Kate, Olivia, and Enzo, taking one for himself as well.

The trip back to civilization seems shorter. They drive through scenic Sicilian villages until they reach Alcantara, on the north slopes of Mt. Etna, about 750 meters—just over 2,460 feet—above sea level.

"Oh, this place is gorgeous!" gasps Kate in awe as they drive up a winding path decorated with cypress trees on either side. From the hands-free car phone, Fabio alerts the vineyard they are about to arrive. Coming around a turn on the gravel road, they see a clearing, in the middle of which sits a beautiful stone and stucco farmhouse with a massive golden-wood pergola laden with greenery. The backdrop of vineyards on rolling hills and incredible views showcasing majestic green and purple mountains is breathtaking.

As Fabio pulls the van up to the farmhouse's entrance, the car is greeted by vineyard owners Viviana and Matteo Rinaldo. In their mid-fifties, the Rinaldos are a handsome couple dressed casually in jeans and T-shirts. The Rinaldos know Fabio well and greet him warmly, after which Fabio introduces Kate, Olivia, and Enzo.

Matteo smiles. "Come, let us show you in and around."

"I'm going to be a fly on the wall, only taking video and stills," promises Enzo, looking at Kate and Olivia.

On Matteo's tour through the rows of vines and rooms where the grapes are aged and bottled, he explains how the altitude, volcanic soil, and climate produce intense wines with a long finish and elegant taste—meaning not too bold, fruity, big, or opulent.

"While red grapes dominate the area, we also have white, which do quite well in this terrain. Our leading grape is Nerello Mascalese, an ancient red grape that is considered close to Sangiovese, the leading Tuscan variety, with red fruit flavors and spice notes of cinnamon, rose, and dried herbs. Nerello Cappuccio is another grape of our region that produces a light-bodied red wine likened to a fine Pinot Noir."

After an extensive tour explaining the history of the area, the grapes, and wines, and that he descends from a long line of winemakers, Matteo leads the group to the farmhouse patio.

Under another pergola, topped with flowing greenery that showcases a picturesque view of the surrounding vineyards and mountains, Viviana and her young assistant Lidia have laid out a beautiful table with trays of antipasto: locally produced cheeses, meat delicacies, olives, olive oil, and fresh bread. A wine glass sits by each place setting, one for each course. For the farm-to-table food-and-wine-pairing feast, the primi, or first course—homemade pasta with a fresh tomato-basil sauce—is served, followed by a course of grilled lamb seasoned with fresh herbs and a garden vegetable medley, then a fennel-and-orange green salad with black olives and a lemon juice and olive oil dressing, and for dessert, a lemon torte, cappuccinos and espresso, and a selection of cheeses, fruits, and nuts.

Enzo makes sure to capture video and stills of each dish and course, only stopping the course of events when absolutely necessary to get his best shot.

"I may not have to eat again for a hundred years," exclaims Olivia, laughing and rubbing her stomach at the end of the feast.

Kate chuckles. "I'll second that. Grazie, the meal was spectacular."

After dinner Enzo asks Matteo if he can get more shots in the winemaking rooms, and Bruno accompanies the men. The women, in the meantime, choose to walk to better digest their meal.

"It's been lovely having you here," Viviana tells them.

"The pleasure's been ours," replies Olivia.

"We'd love to get the recipes for the dishes you served, Viviana," states Kate. "Also, we'll be sure to send you a copy of the article for fact-checking before we go to print."

"We'll send you a copy of the edited video story, too," Olivia adds. "Kate, if I forget, please remind me to have Enzo film my close when he gets back from filming in the winemaker's room."

"Will do."

In the farmhouse's gift shop, Olivia opts for a set of six, pretty. hand-painted dessert plates. Kate picks out some beautiful pottery— olive oil dipping dishes. Viviana also insists that Kate and Olivia take a bottle of lemon-rosemary-infused olive oil. While Kate and Olivia peruse other goodies, Kate sees a hand-painted portrait of St. Maria Goretti holding white lilies on a small plate displayed as a piece of art.

"St. Maria Goretti." Surprised to see the plate, Kate examines the work.

Viviana walks to Kate's side. "She's my saint," explains Viviana.

"Really? I just recently learned about her. The mercy and forgiveness she showed to her attacker are inspiring."

"Yet it is what the Lord calls us to do," says Viviana. "For if you forgive other people when they sin against you, your heavenly Father will also forgive you. But if you do not forgive others their sins, your Father will not forgive your sins. Matthew Six, verses Fourteen and Fifteen."

"Yes," agrees Kate.

"I love this plate because I had to forgive someone who wronged me."

The look on Kate's face tells Viviana she needs to explain. "My late husband—before I met and married Matteo—cheated on me and had a child with another woman. A one-night stand, but a child resulted nonetheless."

"Oh, I'm so sorry—"

"I was too, at the time, and angry. I stayed married to my husband until the end, but it took me many years to forgive him, and at first I didn't want anything to do with the child, a little boy. My husband was very remorseful, though, and I did love him. So my heart softened when I heard about St. Maria and her story of forgiveness—even to the point of wishing that her assailant spend eternity with her in heaven and how the pardon she granted eventually led to her killer's redemption. It made me think a lot about forgiveness of all kinds, and with prayer and time, I could forgive fully."

"And the child?"

"A beautiful boy whom I learned to love because I loved my husband and because the boy was innocent. He's a man now, but we keep in close contact. He's wonderful."

Viviana's story has Kate a little emotional. She starts to tear up."

"Oh," says Viviana, hugging Kate. "I didn't mean to upset you."

"It's a beautiful, touching story. Thank you for sharing it with me. I feel honored."

Viviana hugs Kate again, after which she wraps one of the plates with the image of St. Maria for Kate to take with her.

"I'm going to make up a gift bag for Fabio and Enzo to take with them," announces Olivia. "And I'd love to purchase these items for some of my friends." Olivia hands a basket to Viviana.

"I'd like to get a few more things too," chimes in Kate.

A short time later, Fabio, Enzo, Kate, and Olivia board the van.

"Grazie! *Arrivederci*!" Shouts emanate from the van as it pulls away from the farmhouse. Viviana and Matteo smile and wave until their new friends are out of view.

"What happened in the gift shop?" whispers Olivia to Kate as they head back to the resort in Taormina. The two ladies sit in the van's back seat, Fabio and Enzo in the front.

Kate relates the story of St. Maria Goretti to Olivia and how she first saw a photo in a Taormina restaurant. "And you're not going to believe this," adds Kate.

"Try me." Olivia is all ears.

"Today, I see the image of St. Maria on a plate." Kate removes the plate wrapped in tissue paper from the gift bag and shows it to Olivia. "Viviana explained how St. Maria inspired her to forgive her first husband—who died long before she met Matteo—after he cheated on her. Although very remorseful, things worsened when they discovered that the woman he cheated on was pregnant."

"Oh, brother." Olivia rolls her eyes.

"Well, Viviana prayed and eventually was able to forgive. The toughest part was accepting the child, a boy, which she eventually did and now loves."

"Wow."

"I know, right?"

"You must have been touched. I saw you crying, but I didn't want to intrude."

"Thank you, it would have been okay, but I think I teared up because I haven't quite been able to forgive—myself for the loss of our child, or Kai for Noah. I'm still so emotional."

"It's essential for your recovery to forgive yourself for what may feel like a failure to do what, as females, our bodies are uniquely designed for." Olivia reaches for Kate's arm. "Kai also made a mistake, one he tried to correct for himself, but too late—"

Kate nods. "I know. And Noah is innocent. He didn't ask for any of this. He seems like a fine young man. God must have brought him into our lives for some reason, right?"

"For I know the plans I have for you," Olivia recites the Bible passage found in Jeremiah 29:11.

Kate nods again then looks out the window for a time, lost in her thoughts.

Later that evening, in the resort suite, after Olivia retires to her bedroom, Kate records the day's events and thoughts in her diary, closing with, *Maybe I can learn to accept and love Noah like Viviana did her late husband's child.*

34

"Annabella!" Costanza Costa calls as she enters her daughter's chambers. "Annabella!" Costanza, dressed for the evening in a stunning, bejeweled, pale-blue evening dress, notices the French doors to the terrace are open. She finds Annabella at her easel, painting. "You're not dressed yet?"

"Oh, Mamma, do I have to attend?"

"Yes, yes, you do. Your father will be distraught if you don't. It will be a lovely dinner party, you'll see. Good food and conversation with old friends and your father's associates will cheer you up." Costanza kisses the top of her daughter's head.

Annabella sighs, resigned. "Okay, if you insist."

"I do. Now let's get you dressed."

When Costanza and Flora finish dressing Annabella, she looks like a royal princess. The pale-pink, off-the-shoulder silk dress, adorned with tiny rosebuds about the skirt, shows Annabella's beautiful hourglass figure and small waist to perfection. The dress, and Annabella's hair, pulled up and back with jeweled combs and cascading down her back in long rows of curls, create an elegant, feminine image.

When Annabella and Costanza reach the drawing room, many guests have already gathered. Annabella's father, Antonio, greets his daughter and wife with kisses, introducing them to business associates they have not previously met.

Annabella does her best to be gracious and smile, although she now finds it somewhat painful to be in public. She used to love gatherings like these, but since Stefano's death the previous year, she has not had the stomach to spend much time in idle conversation or wearing a happy façade. She heads out to the terrace to escape her misery and for some sea air.

Then she sees the back of a man standing alone by the terrace railing, looking at the sea. Sensing a presence, the man turns around.

It's Giovanni! Anabella's heart skips a beat.

"Annabella!"

Giovanni walks towards her. "It's so good to see you." He takes her gloved hand and kisses it.

"I had no idea you'd be here tonight."

"I ran into your father several days ago in town, and he invited me."

"Is your wife here?"

"You don't know?"

Annabella looks at Giovanni questioningly.

"She passed away."

Annabella gasps. "When?"

"Two years ago. Consumption."

"Oh, my, I hadn't heard. I'm deeply sorry for you and Lorenzo."

"I appreciate that. I'm sorry for your loss as well. I hope you received our condolences."

"Your card was lovely. Now I understand why only you and Lorenzo signed it. I'm sorry, I just didn't know."

"You had your troubles. I understand Stefano was very sick for quite some time before he passed."

"Yes, consumption as well."

Seconds later, a cheerful Antonio appears on the terrace, disrupting the intense mood. "Dinner is served. Come, you two." Antonio takes his daughter's arm, and the threesome returns inside to join the other guests.

Antonio shows Giovanni to a seat next to Annabella.

Giovanni pulls the chair out from the table, helps Annabella to sit. "You look lovely tonight," he says, sitting down in his own chair.

Annabella smiles demurely. "Thank you."

"Lorenzo will be delighted to learn I saw you."

"He's how old now?"

"Fourteen," replies Giovanni before Annabella can calculate Lorenzo's age.

"Oh my."

Giovanni pulls a pocket watch from his breast pocket. He opens it and shows Anabella a portrait of Lorenzo.

"He's so handsome! Does he still enjoy painting?"

"It's his favorite pastime. He's quite good, I might add."

"He was then, too. And you, your painting?"

"Going very well. My father has many clients who have commissioned paintings from me. And of course, as my most keen admirers, my paintings are displayed throughout my parents' villa," replies Annabella with a chuckle.

"You'll have to give me a tour."

Annabella nods and gazes once again at the portrait of Lorenzo.

"He's a good son," Giovanni says proudly.

"I'm sure. You're his father."

With the ice now broken between the admirers, the rest of the evening is pure magic. "Might I ask you to share dinner with me one night?" Giovanni asks Annabella privately before leaving the Costas' villa.

Annabella blushes. "I would like that very much."

Giovanni takes her hand and kisses it. "Until then."

Later that night, Annabella writes in her diary.

Dear Diary,

Oh, the Lord works in mysterious ways! Tonight, at a dinner party I dreaded to attend, who should be invited but Giovanni Ricci! It's been seven years since I last saw him. He still possesses the same handsome face, physique, and gentlemanly way. How is it that he still has the power to take my breath away? I dearly loved my Stefano and have mourned him so. He was not second best to me, but a wonderful husband. How is it then that I can feel so much for Giovanni? I put him out of my mind the last time I saw him. While it is true that seven years ago Giovanni and I admitted our attraction, we knew it could never be. He was married with a son. We both knew it would devastate our families to be together. And, more importantly, it was wrong in God's eyes—thou shall not commit adultery—the seventh of the ten commandments. I dare not think too far ahead of what might be in the future now. However, it has been a very long time since I have had such feelings of peace and well-being as I do tonight.

I must admit I am also looking forward to the possibility of seeing Lorenzo. He has grown into a handsome young man. We developed an affinity toward each other when I gave him his painting lessons years ago. I wonder how much he remembers of me?

I am committing myself to let things unfold naturally with

Giovanni, and whatever God's will, will be. However, tonight, I do feel in my heart, and with my intuition, that I could fall deeply in love with Giovanni, and if Lorenzo is anything like he was at seven, I will love him as if he were mine and with all my heart.

Annabella

35

Taormina, Province of Messina, Italy, Present day

The day following Kate and Olivia's tour of Mt. Etna and the visit to the Rinaldo Vineyards, the two friends rise several hours later than their usual wake-up times. Kate ties her silk robe with one hand and holds her cell phone in the other as she makes her way into the great room connecting her suite to Olivia's. Light pours in from the open drapes, and a cool breeze blows in through the open French doors. From where she stands, Kate can see Olivia sitting at the terrace table, sipping her coffee as she scrolls through her phone's email inbox. The aroma of coffee brewing in the great room's kitchen is intoxicating, and it's Kate's first stop.

"Morning," calls out Kate, loudly enough that Olivia can hear her.

"Morning."

"I'll be right out. Just grabbing some coffee." Kate pours herself a large mug and tops it off with a tad of cream. "How'd you sleep?" Kate asks as she walks onto the terrace and takes a seat opposite Olivia. She places her phone on the table next to her.

"Like a log. That hike yesterday, all that fresh air, food, and excitement . . . When my head hit the pillow, I was a goner."

"Me too." Kate takes another sip of her coffee, and then her phone rings. The number on the caller ID reveals Rosa is calling. "I have to take this, Olivia. I'll be off in a minute."

Rosa shares her latest findings from Annabella's diary and reads several excerpts to Kate.

"Thank you, Rosa. I look forward to hearing more. Kai and Olivia's husband, Grant, are coming in tonight. We all look forward to joining you for dinner Sunday. Love you, too."

The deer-in-the-headlights look on Kate's face clues Olivia in that something is up. "Tell me what you're thinking."

"I'm processing." Kate takes another sip of coffee. "Rosa just dropped a bombshell—Annabella had a thing with another man before she married her first husband?"

Olivia's interest is definitely piqued. "Oh, please share."

"Annabella's first husband, Stefano, died of consumption a few years after he married Annabella. Annabella was devastated, as she had loved Stefano deeply; they grew up as kids together. However, before Annabella married Stefano, she was strongly attracted to another man, Giovanni, who is *my* fourth-great-grandfather. At the time, Giovanni was married with a seven-year-old son named Lorenzo.

"Wow!" gasps Olivia. "That's quite a confession."

"Their attraction, which happened organically and was not anticipated, was strong. However, Anabella and Giovanni made a conscious decision not to have an affair, as they knew it would destroy their families. Well, it turns out that Giovanni's wife died of consumption a year before Stefano died of the same disease. Cut to a year after Stefano died. Annabella's parents hosted a dinner party to which Giovanni was invited after a chance meeting with Annabella's father, and apparently, Annabella's and Giovanni's passion was reignited. The rest is history. They soon married and had two children, my third-great-grandfather, Leonardo, and his sister, Sienna. Rosa is related to me through Sienna.

Olivia whistles, amazed. "That's synchronicity."

"Isn't that something?" asks Kate.

"It was meant to be," states Olivia.

"It was, wasn't it?"

"According to what Rosa tells me from reading Annabella's diary, the beauty and grace she and Giovanni chose to live, their reverence for the Word, and the example they set, was admirable."

"It's not something we see much of these days," Olivia says, caressing her coffee mug before taking another sip.

"That's true. What I find so beautiful about Annabella and Giovanni's story is that they denied themselves something they truly desired for the sake of their commitment, their families, and their faith. It was as if God granted them their special gift, only in his own time and following his law."

"That gives me chills." Olivia shudders, rubbing her shoulders.

"You mentioned synchronicity," says Kate. "Between learning about Annabella and Giovanni and seeing St. Maria Goretti popping up everywhere. I'm wondering if synchronicity is at play here, too."

"How do you mean?"

"Forgiveness and mercy are St. Maria's calling cards, so to speak."

"And?"

"I was led to find Rosa and my Italian family. Rosa shares details about her miscarriages and told me to forgive myself . . . I learn about St. Maria's story . . . and Viviana shares her acceptance and love for her first husband's illegitimate son . . . Giovanni and his first wife had a son, Lorenzo, whom Annabella loved like her own . . . It all causes me to seriously consider my own troubles."

"Forgiveness, love, acceptance—for yourself and others."

Kate sighs deeply. "It's a lot to process."

Later that morning, while Olivia decides to catch up on computer work before Grant and Kai arrive, Kate rides a motorbike to the ocean. Walking along the shore, her favorite place to think, she ponders all the synchronicities. Aware of her many blessings, and perhaps thinking upon all of Viviana's and Annabella's experiences, Kate starts to sob. She sobs so hard that it's impossible to stand. Luckily, there is a private area by some bushes and rocks where she can sit while she lets her emotions pour out. She cries for her lost child and the life they will not share. She sobs, thinking about how she has been short with Kai after learning about Noah. Tears flow for Noah and what he represents: the fact that he is not hers and Kai's, and the fact that he is innocent. She wonders if she might ever love Noah the way Annabella loved Lorenzo, and then she cries more. She knows that life on earth is not perfect. Sometimes, it is messy and painful. Then, one of her favorite Bible passages—Proverbs 3:56—runs through her mind: *Trust in the Lord with all your heart and lean not on your own understanding; in all your ways submit to him, and he will make your paths straight.* And as she continues to ponder this passage, her tears subside, and an intense calm envelops her, filling her with peace.

Feeling clear-headed and renewed, Kate returns to the resort in late afternoon, approximately an hour or so before Grant and Kai are scheduled to arrive.

"Aloha, my love," calls Kai when Kate enters the suite.

"OMG!" Kate screams, running into Kai's arms and engulfing

him with kisses and a bear hug that causes him to fall onto the couch with Kate on top.

"Wow! How come you didn't greet me like that?" Grants winks at Olivia, who laughs out loud, and, following Kate's lead, jumps into Grant's arms and covers him with kisses.

Grant laughs when the kissing stops. "We are a strange bunch."

For the remainder of the afternoon, Kate is glued to Kai's side. She is so happy to see her husband and can't stop caressing him. Now and then she throws her arms around him and kisses him. Later that afternoon, in the privacy of their suite, Kate nuzzles her head into Kai's chest and again wraps her arms around him.

"I like this new you," says Kai, kissing the top of Kate's head as they stand in their suite's seating area.

"*New* me?" Kate looks questioningly.

"Well, uh, I don't know if I've been one of your favorite people lately."

"Oh, Kai." Kate starts to cry. "I'm so sorry. I haven't been myself, I know."

"Hey, hey, babe, come here." Kai pulls Kate down to the sofa, where they cuddle and hold hands. As Kate babbles incoherently between sobs, Kai continues to caress her, trying to make sense of what Kate is saying. "Sweetheart, let's just be still. Don't try talking right now. Let's just hold one another."

Kate continues to sniffle as she lies on Kai's chest. The warmth and solidness of his arms around her feel amazing.

He is here. He loves me. How blessed am I?

Kate starts to cry again, but her tears subside after a while in the comfort of Kai's arms.

"Feeling better now?" asks Kai sometime later.

Kate nods without speaking. After few minutes, she's ready to share. "I'm sorry, Kai. I know I've been a little hard to take at times these past few months. I'm sorry I shut you out. It's just that I felt like the miscarriage was my fault. After all, I'm a woman. Women are supposed to be able to have a child . . . somehow, I felt it was my fault."

"It wasn't," says Kai firmly.

"I wanted to have your child so badly. But when we learned about Noah, I didn't know what to do. Here was your biological child, you didn't even know the mother, and she could have your child, but I couldn't." Kate starts to sob uncontrollably.

"Oh, honey." Now Kai is crying. "Please, you're breaking my heart. I feel so bad that you've been hurting so much. It was a shock to me to learn about Noah too."

"I know. And Noah is innocent. I've been so consumed with my own feelings. I feel bad that I haven't been there for you."

"I was surprised to learn about Noah. But you don't have to worry about me. I accept whatever happens in that regard. My main concern has been for you."

"I know we'll try to have another child when the timing is right. It's all in God's hands," says Kate, finding more strength now. "I just love you so much and felt I let you down when I lost the baby."

"You didn't. It sometimes happens, my love."

"But I know I let you down with regard to Noah."

"It's been challenging for us both. I felt like I betrayed you somehow. It's been killing me."

"You didn't. It happened before our time." Kate holds Kai tightly. "Remember I told you about how Rosa introduced me to St. Maria Goretti?"

Kai nods as Kate runs her fingers through his silky hair.

"Rosa told me she had two miscarriages and that St. Maria and her story helped her to forgive herself. Olivia and I also met a woman on our food-and-wine tour the other day who shared her story about how she learned to love her late husband's child. Even Annabella loved her husband's son, Lorenzo, like her own. So it got me thinking that I need to give Noah a chance. From my meeting with him that once, and from what you've shared, he seems like such a nice young man."

"He does seem to be."

"Did you have dinner with him while I've been gone like you said you might?"

"His plans changed. Noah said he'd be able to visit Kauai again later in the month. We'll be back from our trip by then. I didn't want to make any plans to meet before I spoke with you because, if you're up to it, I'd like to have you with me."

"I'd like that very much."

Kai kisses Kate tenderly and they hold each other in silence until it's time to get dressed for dinner. "We'll take it one step at a time, okay."

"As long as we do it together," says Kate.

36

Taormina, Province of Messina, Italy, 1875

Annabella' Diary, 1875:

 Today, I married my heart. As I write upon this page, my love, Giovanni, sleeps. It is the middle of the night, and I am still too excited to rest. It is no use. So as not to wake my sweet, I am writing by candlelight in the great room of our new home, Villa del Mare. Selling each of our prior homes to purchase this lovely home in Taormina was the best idea. Giovanni and I could enjoy decorating it to our mutual tastes, tending to every detail together. There is still so much work to do, but we are finally together. I am so happy that I will wake up seeing his face and hearing his voice every day for the rest of our lives. It is bliss. I am so thankful to God that I have been blessed with two great loves in my life. My love for Stefano is not diminished by my love for Giovanni, for Stefano is still in my heart and thoughts, as I believe he will always be. The difference is, when I think about him now, I smile instead of feeling sorrow. Giovanni has helped me gain perspective, and I hope I have done the same for him.

 Lorenzo is a joy. His wit and humor bring so much happiness into our lives. He was delighted to learn that his father and I were planning to marry, and today, he served as his father's best man. His speech at our wedding reception, welcoming me as a loving mother, brought me to tears. My heart is whole. Now I must say my prayers for a beautiful life surrounded by the love of my family and friends.

Annabella

Taormina, Province of Messina, Italy, Present Day

"*Salute!*" La Famiglia—Luigi and Rosa, their children, grandchildren, and other extended family, along with Kate, Kai, Olivia, and Grant—toast before beginning to eat the excellent dinner prepared by Rosa.

"Make sure you save room for six more courses," whispers Kate to Kai.

"Six more?"

"Primi, usually a pasta; *secondi*, a meat or fish dish; and *contorni*, vegetables; *insalata*, a salad; *formaggi e frutta*, cheese and fruit; and *dolce*, dessert. Actually, seven if you count *contorni*, although the secondi or entrée is usually served with contorni—vegetable sides—simultaneously."

"Wow."

Grant laughs, overhearing Kate explain the never-ending course descriptions to Kai. "Should I unbuckle my pants now?"

"Don't you dare," scolds Olivia playfully. "I'd die of embarrassment. I, for one, will pace myself, as a lady should."

"Got it." Grant nods in understanding. "I promise to behave myself." He kisses Olivia on the lips.

"*Mangiare!*" directs Luigi as he gestures wildly, waving his arms when the first course, *linguine frutti di mare*—linguine with shrimp, scallops, and calamari in a white wine-tomato basil sauce—is presented.

"Kai, more prawns?" asks Rosa, holding a serving tray of the giant red sea creatures dressed in fresh lemon juice and olive oil.

Kai looks at Kate.

"It's your stomach," she says with a laugh.

"A few more. Grazie, Rosa."

"That's what I like to see, a man with a good appetite."

"My appetite must be something to do with fresh Italian air," whispers Grant to Olivia. "I'll have a few more as well, Rosa."

"Remember the pants, Grant," Olivia chides playfully.

"Like you, I'm pacing myself. It's all about the pacing." Grant winks.

After the meal, as Kate and Olivia help Rosa set up trays of dessert and coffee in the kitchen, Kate hugs Rosa.

"Bella, is everything okay?" asks Rosa.

"Si. I just love you. And I want to thank you. For everything I've learned from you on this trip, not just for dinner."

"Of course."

"I had a breakthrough. It happened before Kai arrived. I had a meltdown. However, after our talk, and you sharing your experiences with me, the history of Annabella and Giovanni, and meeting Viviana, I was able to release the pain, forgive myself, and let go of any hurtful feelings I had toward Noah."

"Oh, my dear, that is wonderful."

"I am forever grateful." Kate hugs Rosa again. "I hope you, Luigi, and the family will come and visit us in Kauai."

Rosa chuckles. "I don't think you'll have to pull anyone's leg. Ti amo." Rosa kisses Kate's head.

"Ti amo."

For the next two weeks, Kate and Kai tour Sicily with Olivia and Grant, and then the couples separate for their final week abroad. Olivia and Grant spend time in Rome, and Kate and Kai relax on the Amalfi Coast, after which they head for a short layover in New York before returning to Kauai.

"A happy family is made with many ingredients, the most important of which is love."

--Maryann Ridini Spencer

37

"It was one for the books, Poppy," says Kate as she shows her father the many photos she took in Italy, pointing out the various family members and beautiful locales. The two are sitting on the Weke cottage's great room sofa.

"I'm happy that you're so happy," says Glen. "The trip did you and Kai good."

Kate nods. She doesn't share all the intimate details, but she knows her father can see that she and Kai are back on track.

"Are you good with meeting Noah for dinner tonight?" asks Glen.

"Yup." Kate nods.

From her positive response, Glen can see she truly is at peace. "Good. Let me know how it goes."

"Kate, hon, ready?" Kai asks as he enters the great room.

"Ready." Kate stands. She wears a pretty Hawaiian-flower-inspired patterned sundress and strappy sandals.

"You look gorgeous," Kai compliments.

"So do you." Kate smiles as she looks at his cream-colored linen pants and a Tommy Bahama shirt. "We may be home late, Dad. So don't wait up."

"Oh, I've had a busy day at the Plumeria Café market. So I'll get into my jammies and do a little reading, but I'll be turning in early."

"See you for breakfast then." Kate kisses her father on the cheek, and she and Kai leave for dinner.

Sitting alone at a quiet table at one of the local hot spots, Kate notices that Noah looks a bit nervous as she and Kai approach his table.

"Aloha," Noah greets them.

Kate and Kai sit, and the three exchange pleasantries.

A waiter takes their drink orders and hands them menus to review. "I'll return in a few minutes to take your dinner selections," he

187

says before he departs.

"How have your studies been going?" Kai asks Noah.

"Very well. I aced my finals this term. I'll be doing an emergency medicine internship at The Queen's Medical Center in Honolulu over the summer and fall.

"Fantastic," congratulates Kai.

"That's wonderful, Noah," adds Kate.

"It's nice to see you both," Noah admits somewhat shyly.

Kate can't help but get the sense that he is a kind soul.

"I know how awkward this has probably been, learning about me," Noah continues.

"To be honest, it has been . . . a revelation," Kai admits.

"Yes, it has been. You're courageous, Noah. Delving in and reaching out, it takes guts," says Kate.

"I think that, after my mom passed, I just wanted to know more about where I came from, my roots, so to speak. I was curious. I want to say right up front that I just wanted to meet you both. I'm not looking for anything more. I appreciate you're both willing to meeting with me."

"I understand what it is to want to know one's roots. Over the past few years, I've researched my mother and father's family trees and made some fascinating discoveries," Kate tells him.

"Really? I'd love to hear about it. Do you feel comfortable sharing?" asks Noah.

Talking about their families, life's challenges, and discoveries, helps Kate, Kai, and Noah find common ground. They converse until it's nearly closing time. Then, when Noah leaves the table for the men's room before they leave, Kate and Kai agree to invite Noah to their house several nights later. They will make it a family night and invite Kai's father, Bradford, sister, Malie, and brother-in-law, Aukai, to join them for dinner at the Weke cottage.

At home later that evening, as they get ready for bed, Kate sits on the bathroom's vanity chair, taking off her makeup, while Kai brushes his teeth.

"He's a good kid," says Kate, removing her eye shadow with a cleansing towelette.

"He is."

"I like the fact he's so honest. No pretenses. I can understand why he wanted to meet us."

"Are you really okay with having Noah over for dinner to meet the rest of the family?"

"Yes, I am." Kate stands and walks over to Kai. "Maybe we can all be friends."

Kai brushes his wife's hair away from her face, looking lovingly into her eyes. "You're quite amazing. You know that?"

Kate just smiles.

"I love you," he says.

"Ti amo." Kate whispers and kisses Kai's lips.

Several nights later, as planned, with Malie's help, Kate sets the lanai dining table while Kai, Aukai, Glen, and Bradford tend to the fish on the grill.

"I'll get it," calls Kate when the front doorbell rings.

Malie, meanwhile, continues to lay out the antipasto trays.

"Aloha." Kate greets Noah at the front door. "These are gorgeous, mahalo," she says when Noah hands her a lovely assortment of tropical flowers in a basket. "It's the perfect arrangement for our dining table tonight. Come in and follow me."

Noah follows Kate out onto the lanai.

"Aloha, Noah. Let me introduce you to everyone." Kai proceeds to introduce Noah to the family.

"Can I get you a drink?" offers Bradford.

"Soda with a twist of lime would be great right now," says Noah as Bradford fetches a glass.

"Just so everyone knows," announces Kate, "tonight, Kai and I will be presenting you with an authentic Italian dining experience."

"Kate's been cooking all day," Kai says with a chuckle. "So get ready for a night of feasting. There will be seven courses."

Everyone on the lanai tries to speak at once. "Seven courses!" "What?" "Are you kidding?"

"That's how they do it in Italy," exclaims Kate. "Besides, I was anxious to make some of the family recipes Rosa provided."

"I can't wait to sample them. Maybe we might want to put one or two of the dishes on the menu at the Café," suggests Malie.

"Noah, I hope you like to eat. That's what we do here at the Weke cottage. Party all the time." Glen pats Noah on the back as they head to their seats at the dining table.

"I think I can handle it." Noah chuckles. "At least I'll give it the ol' college try."

"That's my boy," Glen says with a laugh.

"You know, Malie, I have a new idea to add to our next Nā Pīkake fundraiser," says Kate in the kitchen with Malie as they place the first course, a homemade pasta topped with seared scallops and a garlic-lemon-butter sauce, in a large ceramic bowl.

"What's that?"

"We've been discussing fostering family relationships through communication and understanding. So, what if we add in the 'how'— *healing through forgiveness*?"

"I like it!" enthuses Malie. "Forgiveness is essential in building healthy, strong relationships."

"Maybe a weekend workshop of sorts, taught by professionals," suggests Kate.

"Culminating in a celebratory meal like this," adds Malie. "Brilliant, Kate."

"Hands, please," says Kai once everyone is seated around the table. Each of them holds the hands of the people next to them while Kai says grace. "Mahalo, our heavenly father, for this nourishing food lovingly prepared by Kate for us to enjoy tonight. We thank you for this bounty that sustains us and the blessings of our family who surrounds us.

E hoʻomaikaʻi aku i ke Akua Makua, ke Keiki a me ka Uhane Hemolele.

Praise be to God the Father, the Son and the Holy Spirit. Amen.

The Ricci Family Tree

Kate Grace's family

1868—Annabella Costa and Giovanni Ricci meet (Giovanni's son, Lorenzo, is seven years old)

1868—Annabella and Stefano Bianchi marry

1872—Regina Ricci dies

1874—Stefano Bianchi dies

1875—Annabella marries Giovanni Ricci (Lorenzo is fourteen)

1876—Annabella and Giovanni have a son, Leonardo Ricci

1877—Annabella and Giovanni have a daughter, Sienna Ricci

1897—Sienna Ricci marries Aldo Lombardi

1898—Sienna and Aldo have a daughter, Lucia Lombardi

1900—Leonardo Ricci marries Anna Maria Costello

1901—Sienna and Aldo Lombardi have a son, Armondo Lombardi

1901—Leonardo and Anna Maria Ricci have a son, Gitano Ricci

1909—Leonardo, his wife Anna Maria, and son, Gitano, move to Boston and open a grocery

1920—Gitano Ricci marries Lucia Campanile

1922—Gitano and Lucia Ricci have a baby boy, Leo Ricci

1941—Leo Ricci marries Mary Rossi

1949—Leo and Mary Ricci have a daughter, Catherine (Kate's mother)

1964—Glen Grace marries Catherine Ricci (They have a daughter, Carla, and a son, Derek, before Kate is born)

1987—Glen and Catherine have daughter, Kate

The De Luca Family Tree

Rosa De Luca's Family

1875—Annabella and Giovanni Ricci marry

1876—Annabella and Giovanni have a son, Leonardo Ricci

1877—Annabella and Giovanni have a daughter, Sienna Ricci

1897—Sienna Ricci marries Aldo Lombardi

1898—Sienna and Aldo have a daughter, Lucia Lombardi

1901—Sienna and Aldo have a son, Armondo Lombardi

1920—Armondo Lombardi marries Serifina Gallo

1921—Armondo and Serifina Lombardi have a son, Alfredo Lombardi

1940—Alfredo Lombardi marries Katrina Casella

1941—Alfredo and Katrina have a daughter, Lizette Lombardi

1941— Lizette Lombardi marries Carlo DeLuca

1949 —Lizette and Carlo have a daughter, Rosa De Luca

Photo of Maryann Ridini Spencer by Maria Gregorio-Oviedo

Maryann Ridini Spencer

Writing Aloha

———

Living in wide open spaces surrounded by nature—trees, flowering plants, and desert mountains or coastal seas—is my happy place," says Spencer. "Feeling nature's positive and healing energy inspires me to be creative, intuitive, and empowered."

"I appreciate "Living The Way" or in "The Spirit of Aloha,"

whether I'm on the Hawaiian Islands or in another environment.

Living *Aloha* means living with love, respect, kindness, compassion, and understanding for everyone in our human *ohana* (family). I feel a vital part of our journey here on earth is to find the humanity in each other, love one another, and help each other learn, heal, and grow. If we incorporate God's teachings in our hearts, thoughts, and actions, we can all contribute to making this world a better place."

Maryann Ridini Spencer writes themes of Aloha, penning award-winning novels and writing and producing critically acclaimed projects for film and television. She began her career as a producer/writer for Cable News Network. Later, she was appointed director of publicity for Miss Universe, Inc. She also served as senior vice president of Stephen J. Cannell Productions/The Cannell Studios before founding Ridini Entertainment Corporation. As company president of the award-winning PR, marketing, multimedia-content-creation, and TV-and-film-production company, she is committed to creating, writing, producing, and promoting content that entertains, inspires, educates, and uplifts. She is also a founding partner in the marketing and content creation joint venture, MPowerMedia.

A member of the Writers Guild of America West and Producers Guild of America, Maryann has produced numerous movies and series for television. Her projects have appeared on Showtime, SyFy, TMC, USA Networks, CBS-TV, Time Warner Cable, and in the foreign theatrical market. In addition, she is celebrated for co-producing/writing the teleplay for the Hallmark Hall of Fame movie *The Lost Valentine*. Based on the James Michael Pratt novel, the movie stars Betty White and Jennifer Love Hewitt. Over fifteen million viewers tuned in to watch the film, which won CBS-TV the night in ratings. The film, winner of the Faith and Freedom Movieguide Award, has since become part of Hallmark's Gold Crown (DVD) Collector's Edition, and the film can also be live-streamed on Hallmark's movie channels.

Maryann is also the creator, writer, producer, and host of the Telly Award-winning healthy living cooking series, cookbooks, and blog *Simply Delicious Living with Maryann*. The series is broadcast on

PBS-TV station KVCR in Southern California, DirecTV, DishTV, and to a global audience on Maryann's SimplyDeliciousLiving.com blog:
https://maryannridinispencer.com/simplydeliciousliving

And at Maryann's YouTube Channel:
https://www.youtube.com/MaryannRidiniSpencer

Maryann has worked as a freelance writer and contributing editor for such publications as *Palm Springs Life Magazine, Desert Magazine, Ventura County Star,* and *Los Angeles Magazine*. Author of the *Simply Delicious Living with Maryann®—Entrée* cookbook (Santa Rosa Press, 2019), and the Kate Grace novels, *Lady in the Window* (2017/2019) 2017 Best Book Awards: Fiction: Romance winner, 2018 American Fiction Visionary Award winner, and 2019 Hawai'i Book Publishers Association Ka Palapala Po'okela Awards–*Aloha From Across the Sea* Award Finalist; *The Paradise Table*, 2019, an Amazon bestseller; *Secrets of Grace Manor* (2021) 2021 Best Book Finalist; and her latest, *Under the Tropical Skies* (2022). Maryann is working on new Kate Grace novels and other fiction, cookbooks, and screenplays.

Visit Maryann at:
https://www.MaryannRidiniSpencer.com

Reader Discussion Guide

- Presently, there are several online sites where ancestry can be traced. What do you think about this practice? In *Under the Tropical Skies*, Kate and Kai's relationship faces challenges due to DNA testing discoveries. What are your thoughts about this type of research and locating one's blood relatives?

- Research indicates forgiving ourselves and others for transgressions is essential for our mental, physical and spiritual health. What do you think? Did you ever find difficulty forgiving another or yourself? Why is practicing forgiveness so important?

- Kate and Kai suffer a loss in *Under the Tropical Skies*. Healing comes to them uniquely. How have you healed from past loss—of a person, work situation, or relationship?

- Kate cherishes her morning talks to God. She also makes a habit of praying. Discuss why her relationship with the Divine is vital in her life. What are your beliefs? What role does prayer have in your life?

- Annabella and Giovanni made a sacrifice. Talk about the reasons behind this. What were their motivations? Would those motivations be valid today? If you found yourself in a similar situation, what would you do?

- Our elders, parents, grandparents, uncles, and aunts sometimes give us sage advice based on their own experiences. What have you learned from your elders? Describe your experiences. What are some thoughts, ideas, and understandings you wish to convey to your children and grandchildren?

- The beauty of the Hawaiian Islands and the Garden Isle is a place people liken to paradise. Have you ever been to Hawaii? What appeals to you most about Hawaii? The practice of Living Aloha?

- What part of *Under the Tropical Skies* resonated with you most and why?

- All the Kate Grace novels focus on connection—to family, friends, and community. Is family important to you? What makes a family? What might be ways to foster connection and thoughtful, respectful communication?

www.ingramcontent.com/pod-product-compliance
Lightning Source LLC
Chambersburg PA
CBHW070349200726
48294CB00003B/811